The Hit

MICHAL HARTSTEIN

DEDICATION

This book is dedicated to loved ones who died
prematurely:
Prof. Ami Vansover, R.I.P.
And Idit Moskowitz R.I.P

ACKNOWLEDGMENTS

Many thanks to my Hebrew editor, Rassel Dickshtein, to my English translator, Michal Fram Cohen, Ph.D and to my English editor, Julie Phelps.

I would also like to thank my beloved aunt, Sara Vansover, for her great support.

Special thanks to Prue Thorner for reading the last edition and offering her wise words of advice and for Adv. Hagit Nahmani-Weiss.

CHAPTER 1

Monday, June 13, 2011

The sharp knife skillfully approached the infant's exposed skin. Though I was a touch away from him, I could not save him. This time, I was determined not to avert my gaze, but the moment the knife reached the baby's foreskin, I closed my eyes.

My little brother's first-born son became a Jew.

"And his name in Israel will be −" announced the *mohel*, and Evyatar bent down and whispered the chosen name in his ear, "Daniel, son of Evyatar and Efrat Levinger."

I searched with my eyes for Efrat. She was leaning on her mother near the entrance to the hall. Like most mothers, she, could not bear to watch her son's circumcision ceremony. I could only imagine how a young mother feels when her week-old son undergoes a surgical procedure without anesthesia. I knew that, along with other parenting experiences, I would be spared this.

The ceremony ended and the cluster of guests began

to disperse among the tables. I approached Evyatar and Efrat and hugged them warmly. Efrat was weeping inconsolably. I could not figure out if it was out of excitement or anxiety. The *mohel* gave them some brief instructions and guidelines for treatment, and they took little Daniel away to a side room. I looked at the packed hall. Shira waved at me from a distance. I realized that, to get to her, I would have to pass through scores of relatives and friends eyeing me. At best, I would get the pitiful looks reserved for spinsters - or divorcees, to be exact. Thirty-four-year-old seniors. Worst case – I would be compelled to talk with someone who would insist on giving me a personal blessing, wishing me marriage and fertility. I was already confident that, this time, the guests would be satisfied with eyeing me with compassion, but just before I managed to sit down next to Shira in front of the succulent salmon dish I had ordered, a short, chubby guy stopped me.

"Hadas?!" he half-asked. I smiled in embarrassment. The guy looked familiar, but I could not remember from where.

He came to my rescue. "Dudi Shpigler. We were together in the Youth Movement troop."

"Dudi," I said. I nodded and smiled a pale smile. I did not know what I was supposed to say or do. "What are you doing here?" I asked finally. After all, he was here at my family event.

"I'm Danit's husband," he said. I continued to look at him with a glassy gaze, and he hurried to explain. "Formerly Danit Kraus." He pointed out a skinny girl who was sitting next to Ilan, Evyatar's best friend from high school. She was doubled up laughing. Apparently, Ilan was telling her another of his jokes. "Danit's a childhood friend of Evyatar."

"Ah..." I said and stared longingly at my salmon platter. "I didn't know you'd married Danit." Truthfully, I did not know Danit at all. "I assume you, too, deserve a *Mazal Tov.*"

"For what?" he wondered.

"For getting married."

He burst out laughing. "I remember you always were funny." Remarkably, I did not remember one single occasion when I had joked with my buddies in the Youth Movement. "Sharp as a razor!" he chuckled. "Danit and I have been married for seven years already!" He explained the joke to me.

I smiled. "Sorry, I still didn't know you married Danit."

I tried to sound like someone who had some idea of the lives of those around her. "I don't remember you attending Evyatar and Efrat's wedding."

"That's true... Danit had only just given birth to our third daughter."

I looked at Danit, stunned. If I had it right, she was Evyatar's classmate... twenty-eight years old, already a mother of three - and so skinny!

"How nice," I said, because I had nothing smart to say. In fact, I thought it was anything but nice that a young woman of only twenty-eight had buried herself in an ocean of diapers, milk substitutes and pacifiers, instead of seeing the world and developing herself, but I realized that it was not the right time or place - and not my business.

"I heard you got divorced," he said without blinking.

"Who told you that?" I challenged him.

"Yuval Eidelman. He told me he'd met you near his kids' school." I recalled my weird encounter with Yuval about a year-and-a-half earlier, when I was investigating the Danilowitz family murder and suicide.

"So I was the topic of your conversation?" In my wildest dreams, I would never have guessed that my former friends from the Youth Movement - if it was at all possible to call our common past a "friendship" - were discussing me in their social circles.

"You were definitely the topic of conversation at that time when you cracked that terrible case with Meir Danilowitz. Well done, by the way."

"Thank you."

"You know we held a memorial soirée for Hanni?"

"Yes, I heard about it."

In fact, I had been invited to the event the friends had organized in Hanni's memory, but I managed to get out of it with some excuse.

"Too bad you didn't come. It was very emotional, and there was also a lot of praise for you - for cracking the case." That was exactly the reason I had elected not to attend. "So you're still divorced?" His bluntness amazed me.

"Yes," I almost whispered.

"I'm asking because I've a good friend at work who's also divorced, though it's fairly recent. But it was a long separation." I realized what he was driving at and stole a desperate look at Shira, who reciprocated with an understanding look. I hoped she would find a way to rescue me quickly.

Dudi continued. "I know it's a little strange that I'm trying to get the two of you together like this, but I think it could really work out."

Based on what? I thought to myself. In spite of our common past, we had never exchanged more than two sentences. In fact, we were now conducting our longest ever conversation.

"He's also ex-religious, like you."

Now I understood. Like many others, Dudi thought that ex-religious folks needed a support group. I glanced again in Shira's direction. I realized she was preoccupied with wiping little Eran's face, which was all smeared with ketchup. "Though he already has one kid with his ex-wife, I'm sure he'll want more." Dudi was doing everything to sell me the merchandise.

"So I'm really not for him," I said brightly, and just before I burst into my stock speech on parenthood, Shira finally came to my rescue.

"Your phone's ringing," she said and handed me my ancient cell phone. When the ceremony had started, she had sat down in the back, so I asked her to watch over my phone.

Dudi looked at me, stunned. This was not because I had such an ancient cell phone, but because of the ease with which I had just rejected the dream man he was offering me. "You'll have to forgive me. I must get this," I said without looking at the phone. As far as I was concerned, even a call from a ceiling fan salesman was more urgent than the conversation with Dudi Shpigler. The phone stopped ringing. Dudi's face indicated that he was happy to get a renewed opportunity, but my phone display revealed, to my alarm, ten unanswered calls from Alon, and five more calls from him with abundant exclamation marks. I felt the blood flowing straight to my feet. Dudi and Shira immediately noticed the change in my expression.

Dudi asked, "Is everything alright?"

"Come, sit down!" Shira tried to drag me to the chair.

I looked at my salmon in despair. I knew I would not be enjoying it. "Everything's alright," I said in a voice full of confidence, "but something must have happened, because my commander's left me a million messages."

"So you're leaving?" Shira asked sadly.

"I don't know," I said, though I guessed I was needed elsewhere. Alon had the tendency to categorize almost anything as "urgent," but I assumed he would not call me out of a family function unless it concerned an unusual incident.

I exited the hall into a quiet courtyard and dialed Alon's number.

"Oh! It's about time!" Alon answered in less than a second.

"I'm at my nephew's bris."

"Has he been made a Jew yet?"

"Yes," I said, and could not help smiling. Alon always knew how to get to the point.

"Then get yourself down to Lincoln Street in Tel-Aviv at the speed of light."

"May I ask what happened?"

"Call me from the car."

I returned to the hall. Shira looked at me full of reproach as I retrieved my purse and grabbed a bread roll from the center of the table.

"So all the cops in Tel-Aviv are on vacation, then?" she commented acerbically.

"Very funny."

"Not really."

"Believe me, if it was up to me, I wouldn't leave, but I don't work in an ordinary job, for better or worse."

"Alright, alright," she said. "I suggest you get out as quickly as possible, before mom, notices you leaving so early."

She was right. Unfortunately, it was too late. The moment I turned to leave, I saw our mom walking toward us. She was looking straight at me.

"You're leaving?" she asked without the reproachful tone I always expected to hear from her in that situation. I was confused. I was expecting a chastising lecture. I nodded soundlessly.

"I heard what happened in Tel-Aviv," she told me like a confidante. "I understand you've been called in."

"What happened?" asked Shira and saved me. I still had no idea what it was about.

"There's been a terrorist attack!" my mom announced.

"What? Where?" Shira asked in panic and immediately went to check her cell phone. Mom said that it was in Tel-Aviv and looked at me knowingly. "There's nothing to see," she told Shira. "It hasn't gone public yet."

Shira asked her how she knew about it.

"Efrat's father's office is in Rubinstein House, right next to the location of the attack." I remembered that Rubinstein House was on Lincoln Street. "One of the employees called and said there'd been some explosions and the entire street's full of police."

"I must go," I said and kissed my mom on the cheek. "*Mazal Tov*. Pass it on to Evyatar and Efrat."

"Yes, of course, of course." My mother looked at me, full of admiration. I loved it. With time, she had learned to accept my work and sometimes, like at that moment, I even had a feeling that she was actually proud of me.

"Don't let us delay you," she added and waved me away.

I ran to the car and immediately called Alon.

"How much time, Levinger? How much time..." he gasped. "What was unclear about you getting here at the speed of light?"

"I challenge you to get away from any event of my family in under a minute."

"Are you on the way?"

7

"Yes. Can you update me with some details? I understand there's been a terrorist attack."

"Attack? Why an attack? Who told you there was an attack?"

"Some guests at the bris are connected to people working in a building nearby."

I heard Alon's voice change as he grinned. "Major Rumor didn't check the rumor as he should this time."

"Then there was no attack? People said they heard explosions."

"This is what happens when civilians spread rumors. Shots, not explosions."

"It could still be a terrorist attack -"

"You know the chance of an armed Palestinian getting to the center of Tel-Aviv is zero."

"Then it's a criminal case."

"Most probably. I don't want to talk too much on the phone. When you arrive, you'll see for yourself."

When I approached the Ma'ariv Bridge, I had to turn on the siren. The scene of the incident had created a bottleneck of scores of cars in an area usually jammed to begin with. The drivers looked at me accusingly as if I was in a hurry to buy a falafel and was passing them for no reason. When I approached the scene, a uniformed policeman signaled to me where to park the vehicle. I grabbed my bullet-proof vest from the back seat and hurried to the address Alon had given me. I could already see him barking at a rookie who had failed to mark the crime scene properly. When he noticed me, he left the poor guy alone and moved on to yell at me.

"Miss Levinger, do you have *any* idea how long I've been waiting for you here?" Alon flared, not expecting an answer. "Anyone'd think you'd had to hitchhike from the moon. It was just a drive from Kfar Ha-

Maccabiah… ten minutes at this time of day."

Even if the road had been empty, it would have taken twenty minutes. "Traffic jams," I muttered without contesting his faulty time perception.

"Traffic jams?" he said and smiled cynically. I knew he was anything except amused. "How many times do I have to tell you to turn on the siren?"

"I turned it on -"

"I bet you didn't have it on the whole way!" He was right. "But now you're finally here, thank God, we can start."

"Why did you wait for me at all?" Why And, like in all great tragedies was I so important?

"You'll understand right away," he said and headed for the crime scene. "Today, around twelve-thirty - lunchtime - a man armed with a handgun stood in front of a snack bar called Zelda and shot at it. The front window of the snack bar was entirely shattered, two individuals were killed and three more were wounded and taken to the hospital in moderate to severe condition." He signaled me with his hand to enter the snack bar.

"And the shooter?"

"He escaped from the scene on a motorcycle."

It was a small snack bar, crowded at the time of the shooting, which explained the multitude of injuries. One of the waitresses was sitting at a table inside, crying incessantly, while a policeman was trying in vain to question her. The central counter, close to the shattered windowpane, was covered entirely with splinters of glass and splattered blood. There was an uneaten dish on the counter, and, underneath it, a young woman was lying in a pool of blood. We edged past an aluminum rod that, not long ago, had formed part of the frame of the front window, and advanced further into the snack bar. It was small and had four small tables. Two tables were empty. On the furthest table was a half-eaten breakfast. Chairs were scattered across the floor. Whoever had been sitting on them had either fallen off or run for his life. By the table attached to the counter, the body of the second fatality was spread out. Based on the position of the body, I assumed he had been sitting when the shooting started; he had jumped up in surprise, and had immediately been shot, falling next to the table.

Alon approached the table and stood next to the body. He signaled to me to approach him.

"Does he look familiar to you?" he asked and pointed at the body.

I knelt down. The dead man lay on his stomach, his head turned sideways, his open eyes looking at me with a hollow stare. Thin flow of blood from his gaping mouth had accumulated in a red puddle around his face.

It took me a few seconds to realize that I knew the guy.

It was Koby Ozri, my principal informer.

CHAPTER 2

Koby Ozri came from a large traditional family from Pardes Katz. His parents, burdened by providing for their eight children, did not notice when their fifth child was drawn into the world of crime. By the time Koby met Oren Hadida, he had never worn a piece of clothing that had not been previously worn by one of his siblings or his older cousins, and he had never played with a new toy.

Oren Hadida was the right-hand man of Ephraim Zuckerman, the head of the notorious Zuckerman gang. Oren was a ruthless, unscrupulous criminal who flinched at nothing to gain what he wanted. He did time for drug and fraud felonies, and it was rumored that he had liquidated at least ten people with his own hands, two of them actually inside the jailhouse, whilst serving time. Prior to fleeing to South America and joining a brutal drug cartel, he had managed to incriminate his boss, Ephraim Zuckerman, and had instigated the dismantling of one of the best-known veteran gangs in the Tel-Aviv District. Oren's special talent was recruiting new soldiers to the gang's ranks. He knew how to track down the appropriate persons - appropriate being reckless young men and boys suffering physical or mental deprivation.

Koby Ozri was sixteen and one of the easiest to recruit. A new bike and a short visit to a prestigious clothing store bought his trust. At first, Koby had served as a courier, and later as a lookout while other gang members emptied out houses and shops of their valuables. His parents noticed his new clothes and the gifts he showered on his brothers and sisters, but liked to believe their son had earned his money honestly. They kept comparing Koby to a relative from Jerusalem who had grown up penniless, but had accumulated a fortune; he had started trading in the Mahane Yehuda Market at age fifteen, and twenty years later he owned a nationwide supermarket chain. The harsh reality reached their doorstep several weeks before Koby was scheduled to be drafted into the IDF, when he was arrested and indicted for property felonies. Since he was over eighteen, he was charged and sentenced as an adult. And so, while his friends enlisted with various army units, Koby served time with seasoned criminals. When he was released and tried to reform his ways, the army refused to take him. He was compelled to avoid eye contact whenever he met old friends who were often dressed in uniform and decorated with insignia, on home leave from the army base.

His criminal background and the fact that he had not served in the army made it difficult for Koby to find a permanent rewarding job. Within a short time, he was sucked once again into the underworld and joined the Zuckerman gang. Ephraim Zuckerman loved Koby. He realized quickly that Koby was loyal and had a good heart. He also realized that Koby did not have a brutal character, so he refrained from sending him on violent missions. Still, he knew that he could count on Koby to take the secrets he had seen and heard to his grave.

After Oren Hadida betrayed Ephraim Zuckerman and fled to South America, the gang was dismantled. Ephraim Zuckerman collapsed and died during his trial. Many gang members were sentenced to long terms in jail. Koby also served another two years because a handgun that had been used in a murder committed by another gang member had been found in his backyard.

Over the years, the gang members forged new loyalties and found other gangs, but not Koby. He desperately missed Ephraim Zuckerman and thought that if he joined a new gang, he would be disloyal to his beloved mentor. He was also very hurt by Hadida's betrayal and found it hard to regain his trust in people. He didn't leave the crime world, but started to provide his services as a seasoned criminal to anyone: he became a freelancer of the underworld. He was known to many criminals, as well as to the police. Many, even among the ranks of the police, held him in high regard because of his near mystical relationship with the late Ephraim Zuckerman.

A year-and-a-half before his body was found in the Zelda snack bar, Koby had become one of the central, most productive informants I had ever managed to recruit. Over the years, Koby had learned to be extremely careful, but he was caught in a warehouse where stolen goods were found, purely by accident. A couple conducting an after-hours affair late at night in a nearby building noticed suspicious movements in the warehouse and called the police. Until the cops arrived on the scene and discovered the warehouse's contents, nobody in the Israeli Police Department had known about its existence. That night, I was on duty, and when

Koby was brought to the police station, I was asked to interrogate him.

When I entered the room, Koby was sitting, head down. His caution and meticulousness had kept him out of the interrogation room for many years. I knew he was a seasoned interrogee, and that my chances of drawing any information out of him – someone who had been known for years as one of the most loyal of gang members – was nil.

I read him the details of the case as summarized by the patrolmen. Koby barely raised his eyes. I tried to make him talk, but he was simply silent. After half an hour, he opened his mouth and asked for a glass of water. I went to the hallway and brought him a glass of water. When I gave him the glass he finally raised his eyes and, from that moment, did not take his eyes off me.

He broke his silence again and asked, "Aren't you the one who caught that pedophile from Givat Shmuel?

I did not know what to answer. I had never spoken to a suspect about another investigation.

"*Nu*... the religious, fat one..." He tried to refresh my memory of the big case I had cracked several weeks earlier.

"Yes, that was me," I answered impatiently. "How's that related to what I asked you?"

His eyes kept drilling right into mine. Now I noticed they were moist. My irritated look changed into a compassionate one. A flow of tears began to roll down Koby's face.

"Do you want more water?" I asked carefully.

"Please..." he sniffed.

I returned to the interrogation room with a new glass of water and a box of tissues. Koby wiped his nose and drank slowly.

"I'm an admirer of yours," he said when he had finished drinking. "Really, really an admirer."

"Thank you," I said. I knew that even among criminals, sex offenses against children were considered immoral and disgusting, but I suspected he was complimenting me because he had known one of the victims of the pedophile I had caught. Perhaps it had been even a relative. I knew that Koby's family was religious and resided in Pardes Katz, a neighborhood next to Givat Shmuel.

"What those children went through..." he said and lowered his gaze. His speech halted until he managed to say in a whisper, "I also went through it."

This was unexpected. "When?" I asked.

"When I was a young kid, maybe nine or ten."

"Who was it?"

"It was the principal of the school I went to," he said and pursed his lips. His chin started to tremble. I was afraid he was about to burst into tears again.

"Are you alright?" I asked with concern.

He nodded and regained his composure. "It was a Haredi school for boys in Bnei Brak. My parents weren't very religious, but they thought I'd get a better education over there." He smiled a sad smile. "I was a mischievous kid. It was hard for me to sit on my ass, and almost every week I was sent to the principal, who was also a well-known and respected rabbi in Bnei Brak. He raped me dozens of times." Koby could not now hold back his tears. "Dozens!" he repeated almost in a shout. He took a tissue from the box and wiped his tears. "He told me I must be punished, and if I told anyone about his punishments, God would punish me."

"So you never complained about him?"

"No."

"You didn't tell anybody?"

"I told Ephraim Zuckerman, God rest his soul."

"How did he react?" I was curious.

"He didn't say anything after I told him, just sat there silently. I thought he was in shock. I can only tell you that, less than a month later, that rabbi was killed in a strange car accident."

I could not hide my smile.

"Ephraim Zuckerman was like a father to me. I have a father and I love him, but he's weak. He never knew how to stand up for himself. I didn't even consider telling him what the principal did to me. I didn't believe he'd do anything. I admit I told Ephraim because I hoped he'd do something, and, indeed, he did. I knew he wouldn't tell anybody about my shameful secret, and he knew he could count on me a million percent." Koby looked at me through reddish eyes. I was, in fact, the first person to whom he revealed the nature of his intimate relationship with Ephraim.

"I'm a criminal," Koby continued with his monologue. "It's all I know how to do. How would my life have turned out if I hadn't suffered... what I did? Do you know how much of my life I've wasted in jail?" he asked and did not wait for an answer. "A total of six years and ten months. During that time, I read hundreds, if not thousands, of books of all kinds: thrillers, espionage, reference books, I even managed to read a cookbook. I don't have much education, but, believe me, I'm more educated than many people with a degree. If I hadn't suffered what I went through, maybe I wouldn't have got pulled into this world of crime. I'm not particularly proud of it, but I had no other choice."

I looked at him with empathy, but found it hard to

identify with what he just said. He realized that I was not entirely with him.

"I know what you're thinking. That I'm a crybaby and didn't try hard enough, but you don't know what I've gone through, how many times I've tried to rehabilitate myself - but no one's gonna trust someone who's fallen into crime. Did you know I was married and have a fifteen-year-old daughter?"

I looked at his file, which was open before me. The personal details showed: Divorced plus 1.

"Do you know I haven't spoken to my daughter in two years?" Again, he posed a question without waiting for an answer. "I divorced her mother when my little girl was three. I loved her mother deeply. She's an amazing woman. She agreed to accept me in spite of my past, but she said if I ever went back to crime, she'd leave. We were married four years. It was only in the first year that I really stayed away from crime. When my daughter was born, I couldn't look my wife in the eye. I wanted to give everything to her and to my daughter, but with the odd jobs - all I could get - I couldn't give them anything. When my daughter was three, I was arrested for some nonsense and sentenced to one year. Since then, I haven't spoken to the love of my life without some lawyers in the room. She allowed me to see my daughter only under the supervision of social workers, until she reached thirteen. Since then, the girl herself has refused to see me."

He stopped talking and stared at the desk. A small tear dropped from his eye and dropped onto the veneer of the desk. After few seconds, he clenched his fist and hit the desk angrily. I knew the other cop on call was observing us and signaled him that everything was fine. "He destroyed my life!" he shouted. "That son of a bitch destroyed my life!" He looked straight at me again. His eyes were red and full of anger. "Not a day goes by I don't think about it. If that dog hadn't done to me what he did, I wouldn't have turned bad. I could've had a different life today! Maybe I'd have studied something.... maybe I'd have had a good profession, and be living with my wife and my daughter. I feel like I'm living someone else's life, and I'm sick of it..."

I did not open my mouth. At this stage, I felt that any interference, even the smallest, could destroy everything. I realized that the man was ripe and ready to cross the lines. He was not the first, nor would he be the last, to blame others for his life of crime. The circumstances of his life were, indeed, terrible, but the choices he made were his. This was my opinion, but, of course, I refrained from expressing it aloud.

"Ever since Daphna, my daughter, made it clear she didn't want any contact with me, my life's been meaningless. I just keep going, without any interest or will to move forward. Up to that moment, I'd had a dream - to get rich so I could pamper my little Daphna - but she made it clear to me she wasn't interested in getting any dirty money from me." He spat out the word "dirty" as if it was, in fact, dirty.

He became quieter then, as if he was choosing his words carefully. I reminded myself that the man was used to interrogations. "I'm not saying I'm glad you caught me. Nobody likes to fail. But here, I've failed. You caught me red-handed. If you want, I'll confess here and now whatever you want me to. In any case, I don't have any more energy for hiding and running away. I don't mind sitting in jail for the rest of my life. Nothing interests me anymore. I just want my daughter not to be ashamed of her father... it's important to me that you understand that."

"What are you telling me, in fact?" I tried to get him focused.

"You understand very well what I want to say." He took a deep breath. "I'm ready to be a police informer, but on condition that you're my operator. You did for those kids what nobody did for me. I want to work with you."

Over the next few days, Alon watched Koby's interrogation over and over, as if it was an Oscar-winning movie. He would not cease gushing over me and my colossal achievement. Koby was one of the most prominent CIs our unit had recruited recently. Most of the informers were young felons who had gotten into trouble and wanted to avoid jail time. Koby was a veteran, well-connected criminal who was not afraid of jail at all. His motive was a genuine wish to cross the lines and help the police. Koby's line-crossing was Alon's wet dream, and the fact that I was his official operator strengthened my position in the unit.

Koby was a prolific source of information. While he was not very close to any central figure in the underworld, he knew everybody and everybody knew him. He helped us to map the crime families, their multiple connections and their rivalries. Some of this information was already known, but Koby's testimony confirmed with certainty some assumptions we had been forced to make. The most valuable information provided by Koby was associated with the Golan family. For years, Alon had unsuccessfully tried to lay his hands on the brothers David and Ami Golan. The rumors about their shady business had spread all over the district, but they always managed to dodge any interrogation. Koby was laundering money for them, but we did not have enough evidence to indict them for more serious offenses. Alon wanted to get to the core of their illegal businesses, and would not be satisfied with mere money laundering.

Over the last few months we had a breakthrough in the investigation. Ami Golan, the younger brother and the brains of the outfit, started sharing information about drug deals and trafficking in women with Koby. He transferred money to Koby and hinted that the source of the funds was protection money from businesses in Holon. We were very careful when we worked with Koby. We knew that if we were too greedy, Koby's cover would be blown. He was too important to the unit, and sometimes we had to forego arrests and raids in order to avoid getting him in trouble.

Now, as Koby's body lay before me, still and bloody, I realized that, apparently, we had not been careful enough. Someone from Koby's previous world had decided to settle accounts with him.

CHAPTER 3

It was difficult to look at Koby's lifeless body. We had grown very close during the months we had worked together, and I had learned to like him. He had a sophisticated sense of humor and we had soon accumulated our own private jokes, so that it was sufficient for one of us to mention one word in order for both of us to start laughing. He liked the good life - he loved to try out a new restaurant, and often urged me to try the places he had visited. To the best of my memory, he had never told me about the Zelda snack bar. I raised my eyes and looked up at the wall in front of me. The daily menu offered sweet potato quiche and pasta with pesto sauce, a rather banal menu, not like the gourmet dishes Koby liked to try out. I diverted my eyes to the other body lying near the table, under the counter.

"Has the second victim been identified?" I asked Alon.

He looked at a document in his hand. "Shirley Navon, aged 29, from Hod Hasharon, according to her national ID card. She hasn't yet been positively identified, and none of the employees here knew her personally. I assume she is, indeed, Shirley Navon, but we'll have to wait for the body to be identified by a relative in order to be a hundred percent sure."

"Does she have any connection to Koby?" I asked.

"Probably not. According to the employees' testimonies, she was about to pick up this order," he pointed to a brown paper bag lying on the counter.

I went over to the bag and peeked at the white note attached to it: "Shirley – sweet potato quiche and chicken salad." Shirley had been about to pick up her lunch, and maybe a co-worker's lunch, too.

"So she was just a bystander in the wrong place at the wrong time?"

"Unfortunately, this is probably the case," Alon said angrily.

At that moment, two guys with a stretcher walked in.

"Can we now?" one of them asked Alon. It seemed he had been keeping them away until I'd studied the scene.

"Start with the woman," he instructed them. They covered Shirley's body carefully, picked it up, loaded it on the stretcher, and carried her over to their van, which was parked nearby.

"Two policemen are on their way at this very moment to the address on the ID card," Alon updated me. "It's probably Shirley's parents' address."

"Poor things," I whispered.

"Never mind that they kill each other, but to slaughter innocent people like that, this is crossing the line!"

"Don't forget that Koby was one of us, really," I reminded him.

"That's true," he said and looked gloomily at the body lying on the floor.

Tuesday, June 14, 2011

"Less than twenty-four hours after the murderous hit that led to the death of criminal Koby Ozri and bystander Shirley Navon, right in the center of Tel-Aviv, the police have begun an extensive round of arrests among the crime families in the Central District. So far, over twenty persons have been arrested, including the brothers David and Ami Golan, Yaakov Sela and Erez Hasson. In a press conference held by the Inspector General, Police Commissioner Dotan Arbel, he declared a policy of zero tolerance toward crime organizations that do not flinch from hurting the innocent. An unofficial source in the police confirmed to our reporter that the criminal, Koby Ozri, was an active police informer, and that the possibility that his cover had been blown was being investigated. Moshe Navon, Shirley's father, said in reaction to the round of arrests and the words of the Inspector General: "Nothing will bring Shirley back, and it's regrettable that it took her death to lead to such a round of arrests. Such dangerous criminals should be behind bars, not walking around freely on our streets..."

Alon, the "unofficial source," lowered the volume and looked straight at me. "Who've we managed to interrogate since this morning?"

"I interrogated Rami Shomron and Yaron Levi," I said.

"Who are they?"

"Yaakov Sela's pawns."

"Who else?"

"Shachar's interrogating Michael Schwartz right now."

"The one from the Golan brothers' gang?"

"Correct. When do you want us to proceed to the bosses?"

"Only in the afternoon. Tomorrow morning, even. Let them stew a little in their own juice. They already imagine things that Koby told us. So let them fantasize about what we got out of others in the interrogations."

"Okay."

"What about Tom Sela?"

"He was on his way back from abroad when we issued the warrant for his arrest. According to the information we received, he boarded the plane two hours after we issued the warrant. He's expected to be on the ground in the next few minutes.

"Let there be no screw-ups," Alon instructed. "I want him in the same cell with his father."

Tom Sela was a tall, muscular guy who enjoyed plenty of success with women. The gossip columns loved to cover his numerous conquests and photograph him with young models at various events. Two years earlier, he had been discharged from military combat service and, since then, his father had not ceased bragging about him and his contribution to the country. It was important for Yaakov to create a clean image for Tom, so he was strict about involving him only in his legitimate businesses. To our regret, the information Koby had given us was not sufficient to convict Tom of material criminal offenses. It was clear to us that Tom was well aware of his father's criminal businesses, but we couldn't prove that he was involved with them. We hoped that Tom's arrest would have an impact on his father.

"Two patrolmen have already been sent over to Ben Gurion."

"I hope you didn't send the two geniuses who lost Ben Gigi two months ago," said Alon sourly. That affair had embarrassed the police a lot. Rabbi Reuven Ben Gigi had managed to slip away and board a flight to South America a few hours before the police managed to get a warrant for his arrest on suspicion of bribery and fraud.

I smiled without showing my teeth. "Those two were exiled to a remote station in the south long ago. I sent seasoned cops this time."

To be on the safe side, I called one of them to verify the accuracy of the flight details. Three hours later, the two accompanied the handcuffed Tom Sela into the station.

Riki, the station secretary, ran over to my office.

"He's here," she said, blushing.

"Who?"

"Tom Sela," she declared, not quite managing to hide the stupid grin on her face.

"Watch your tongue doesn't fall out of your mouth."

"Wait till you see him," she laughed. "He looks a lot better in real life."

I rolled my eyes, got up slowly from my chair and followed Riki, who almost danced all the way back to the reception area. When I arrived, the two cops I had sent got up from the bench and instructed Tom to stand up and follow them. The two cops were quite tall, but Tom managed to tower over them by at least half a head. He was, indeed, an attractive man.

"You asked us to bring him straight to you," said one of the cops. It was true. Most of those arrested in the case had been transferred directly to the detention cells, but I wanted to interrogate Tom as soon as possible. He was young and inexperienced in interrogations, and I did not want to risk him being coached by his pals. No less importantly, I wanted his father to know that we had already interrogated him.

"Very good," I said and asked them to follow me.

We entered one of the interrogation rooms. I instructed them to unshackle him. I was not concerned he might try anything.

I sat across from him and looked straight into his green eyes. It was his first time in a police interrogation room, and yet he did not show any sign of anxiety or concern. I did not know if his tranquility derived from any coaching he had previously been given, or from excessive self-confidence.

"Tom, did they read you your rights?"

"Yes," he said and answered immediately, "I want a lawyer." He looked at me and smiled with his lips closed. Huge dimples decorated his cheeks. The guy was charm on legs.

Today, it's impossible to judge suspects as guilty or innocent according to their demand to have a lawyer present. Innocent people have seen American thrillers in the movies and know that, without a lawyer, they might get in trouble. It is precisely the experienced criminals who know well enough how to manage without a lawyer's instructions.

However, Tom was not an experienced criminal, and it was clear to both of us that he needed legal instruction. I handed him a phone and he dialed the attorney Hagai Weiss, who had represented his father in most of his interrogations.

Weiss arrived in about thirty minutes and sat with Tom for a long discussion. After an hour, I instructed the cops to return Tom to the interrogation room.

"Hagai isn't coming in with me?" he asked, alarmed. For the first time since Tom had been arrested, he showed the first sign of cracking.

"No way," I said, chuckling.

Now he looked a little less calm. Apparently, he thought that Weiss would speak in his place. Maybe Weiss had explained the severity of the situation to him, and he was concerned about incriminating himself or his father.

"Though I imagine Attorney Weiss has already told

you the chain of events, I want to update you about what we know and why you're sitting here before me."

He nodded.

"On Monday at noon, an anonymous hitman shot dead Koby Ozri, a criminal known to the police, and a bystander named Shirley Navon, at the Zelda snack bar in Tel-Aviv. Did you hear about the case?"

He hesitated for a moment, then said, "Yes, Hagai just told me about it." It was important to him to make it clear with his first answer that he had not been involved in the hit.

"Did you know Koby Ozri?"

He was silent.

"Tom, I repeat - did you know Koby Ozri?"

He continued to be silent.

"Tom, I don't know what Attorney Weiss told you, but let's be clear here: it's better for you to refrain from silence as much as possible. The longer you keep silent, the longer the interrogation will be. I'll help you a little with this question and tell you that we already know that you knew Koby Ozri. Therefore, I'll ask you again - did you know Koby Ozri?"

"Yes," he whispered.

"A little louder. You know we're being recorded."

"Yes," he repeated aloud.

"Did you have business relations with Koby Ozri?"

He stared at me wretchedly. In spite of his impressive size, he suddenly looked like a small, frightened child. I understood. He was concerned that each unnecessary word he said would get him or his father in trouble. I smiled at him and nodded my head slowly, as if to encourage him to open his mouth and talk. It worked.

"Yes, I had the opportunity to work with him sometime."

"Doing what?"

"I help my father manage his supermarket chain." One of Yaakov Sela's legitimate businesses was a chain of five supermarkets in Holon and Bat-Yam. "Koby was one of my suppliers."

"What did he supply?"

"All kinds of things."

"What does that mean? Don't you have a different supplier for each product?"

"Usually."

"But Koby Ozri was a supplier of 'all kinds of things' according to what you're saying?"

"Yes. Mostly vegetables, fruits and textile products."

"Doesn't it seem strange to you, this combination of textiles and vegetables and fruits? Things not related to each other...?"

"I'm not responsible for my suppliers' businesses."

"Why did you work with him specifically?"

"I entered the business a little over a year ago; Koby was already a supplier when I began working in the chain."

"And do you know how he became a supplier?"

"I know he'd worked with my father for years."

"Were you aware of the fact that much of the merchandise Koby was supplying to your supermarket branches had been stolen, or taken from the producers under threat?"

"Absolutely not!" Tom pretended to look shocked. "Everything was legal as far as I was concerned; there were tax receipts for everything."

I chuckled. "Tom, you may be young, but you're not an idiot. A tax receipt doesn't make merchandise kosher. Didn't it seem strange to you that you were getting merchandise from Koby for very low prices?"

"I never checked the prices charged by others."

"Really?" I wondered. "You bought from suppliers without checking if there were cheaper suppliers?"

"Sometimes. But not in Koby's case, because he was a good friend of my father."

"So Koby was a good friend of your father?"

"Yes." Tom lowered his eyes. He realized he had said a little too much.

"Did you happen to meet Koby Ozri outside of work?"

"Yes," he said in an impatient tone. "I told you - he was a friend of my father."

"Where, for instance, did you meet him?"

"I got to see him at family functions, and he also came over sometimes for dinner at the weekend."

"Did you know that he was a criminal?"

"I knew he'd done time."

"What other business did he have with your father?"

"I've no idea." I did not know if he had any idea or not. What I did know was that there was no chance he would tell me about it.

"How did the relationship between your father and Koby appear to you from the outside?"

"What do you mean?"

"Were they close? Did they care about each other?"

"I don't know... I think they were."

"Were what?"

"Yes, they were close; my father cared about him because he didn't have any close family."

"Did you know that Koby Ozri was a police agent?"

"I heard about it on the news."

"And before it was on the news, did you hear anything about it?"

"Absolutely not!" He was resolute.

"Do you know Haim Aloni?"

"I heard about him."

"What did you hear?"

"He once worked in my father's supermarkets."

"He wasn't just an employee, according to what I know. He was the chain manager. In fact, you were his replacement, weren't you?"

"Right."

"Was your father angry when he left?"

"I've no idea; I was in the army then. I imagine he wasn't happy."

"Let me make it easier for you. We had the opportunity to record your father yelling at Haim that he would, one day, regret leaving him."

Tom shrugged, as if to emphasize he had no connection to the story.

"Do you know what's going on with him today?"

"No. I think he moved to the US."

"That's right. Do you know the reason he left the country?"

"I think he hadn't been all that successful in his business."

I chuckled again. "'Not very successful' is an interesting way to present it. He'd left your father's business in order to open a supermarket on his own. Do you know the story?"

"Not really. I told you, I was still in the army at that time."

"So let me refresh your memory: Haim's supermarket had been already prepared for the opening, completely stocked with merchandise, when an anonymous arsonist burned down the supermarket and its contents just a day before the grand opening."

"Could be. But how's that related to me?"

"It may not be related to you, but it's greatly related to your father."

"As far as I know, my father wasn't charged with anything."

"That's true, too. To our regret, we didn't manage to catch the anonymous arsonist. However, it's impossible not to think that it was an astonishing coincidence that Haim Aloni's store specifically was torched after your father had warned him that he'd regret leaving him, and that the same Haim Aloni fled in a panic to the US as a result."

"I've no idea."

"Tom," I took a long breath, "if your father could be that angry with an employee who just left him to open a rival business, can you imagine how angry he'd be with someone who might have informed on him to the police?"

Tom rolled his eyes. "I've no idea!" he said impatiently. "As far as I know, my father never did anything bad to Haim Aloni or to Koby Ozri."

The questioning was complete and I marked a small victory for myself – not that I thought I could extract any real information from him, but I had succeeded in shaking his confidence and making him doubt himself.

I called in the escort cops and they led Tom down to the detention cell where his father, amongst others, was being held.

I ran to Alon's office and together we watched the meeting between Tom and his father. Yaakov Sela was napping on one of the benches. He had spent quite a few years in various prisons during his life, and being held in a detention cell caused him no discomfort. On a different bench, in the farther corner of the cell, a cab driver who had been caught that day with half a kilo of marijuana in his possession lay shaking and terrified. According to him, he had no idea he was transporting a package of drugs. Except for a considerable number of traffic tickets, he had a clean record, and, for him, spending time in the detention cell was a traumatic experience. For Tom, entering the detention cell was not such a simple experience, either. He was hunched over. He had no idea whom he was going to meet in the cell. When the cop accompanying Tom selected the key to the cell from his batch of keys, the cab driver and Yaakov turned to look at the cell door. Tom was led in, and Yaakov rose to a sitting position and stared at his son, shocked.

"Dad..." said Tom in a choked voice, and approached Yaakov. The cab driver looked at them and the look of agony on his face changed to a look of surprise. He had not expected to witness a family reunion right in front of him during an exhausting day of detention.

"Tom." Yaakov extended his arms toward his son and embraced him warmly. Tom had to bend and shrink in order to squeeze into the extended arms. Within seconds, the robust, muscular man turned into a small, frightened boy trying to find consolation in his father's loving and protective embrace. After long minutes, Tom broke away from his father, and the two sat down. Tom's back was to the camera, but his tone of speech made it clear he was crying.

"Dad," he said and snuffled, "I didn't know what to say." Yaakov immediately hushed him and pointed at the camera high up, out of reach, behind his son. Tom turned around quickly and looked up at the camera.

"Are they allowed to do that?" he asked, shocked. "Surely it's an invasion of priv-" Yaakov again did not let his son finish the sentence. He signaled him with his finger to keep quiet. Tom inhaled deeply and rearranged himself on the bench with his back resting against the wall.

"Tell me, how was Los Angeles?" Yaakov tried to encourage his son, and the two engaged in small talk.

Alon was disappointed. While he did not expect Yaakov to let Tom talk while the cameras and listening devices in the cell were on, he hoped that Tom's arrest would make Yaakov crack. But Yaakov showed no sign of cracking.

CHAPTER 4

Wednesday, June 15, 2011

A trail of edgy, honking drivers who had gotten stuck behind a slow garbage truck woke me up early. I had only returned home at three a.m., after a night of interrogations, and had not planned to get up early. I decided to use the fact that I was awake anyway in order to treat myself to a pampering breakfast. I had hardly eaten anything for two days, and knew that the rest of the day would not present too many opportunities for sitting down and eating. I remembered a nice café, not far from the beach, which Koby had recommended to me and I had not yet had a chance to try. To be honest, I had not visited most of the restaurants he had recommended to me. Those restaurants were too expensive for me, and I was not enough of a connoisseur to enjoy them, anyway. But breakfast, even if it was a little more expensive than the average, was something I could definitely afford.

About an hour later, I was sitting and staring at the menu. I wondered how many patrons around me were trying to calculate the profit margins on each dish. In my estimate, it was a hundred percent overpriced. I was too hungry to get up and leave, and I also decided that the breakfast would be a sort of goodbye to a friend. Koby had had nothing but praise for this café and once hoped out loud that one day he could invite me for a good breakfast there. I ordered and went to the restroom. When I returned, I passed by the cake refrigerator. I recalled the cheesecake that Koby had bought me only a week before, a Shavuot holiday gift. I tried to remember if the cake had come from that café. I could not see any in the display cabinet.

"Do you have a baked cheesecake with a vanilla cream layer?" I asked the passing waitress.

"Yes, of course," she smiled broadly. "It's our most popular cake, certainly during Shavuot."

"I don't see any here," I said and pointed at the refrigerator.

The girl surveyed the refrigerator and called the guy standing behind the counter. "Is the cheesecake with vanilla finished?"

"No, no. I just took it out to cut a piece for a guest," he said and put the cake back in the refrigerator.

I had no doubt. It was the definitely the cake Koby had brought me as a present. I decided I would have a piece for dessert, in memory of a friend who would never come back.

"Hadas!" A familiar voice woke me up from my musing. I looked up, and in front of me stood Revital, an old friend of Yinon's and mine, who, as a part of the divorce process, had become mainly Yinon's friend.

"Revital," I said with a false smile. "How are you?"

"I'm doing great! What about you?"

"I'm fine," I answered. "How are Ronen and the kids?"

"Excellent!"

"You have three, right?" I had not spoken to her for over two years; perhaps I was out-of-date by now.

"Yes," she giggled. "That's it! I've completed my mission. I don't have the energy for another kid, though Ronen drives me crazy, saying we only have a short window to have another one...."

I remembered Ronen advising Yinon to dump me since I did not want children, and hoped that three were enough for him; otherwise Revital herself would be under threat of divorce.

"What are you doing here?" I inquired.

"I took the day off... it's my birthday." She smiled.

"Congratulations! How old are you?"

"I'm celebrating my third Bat-Mitzvah today." I reacted with a frozen smile and she hurried to explain. "I'm thirty-six."

"Yes, I see." I quickly switched to a warmer smile. I was still stuck in the horrible memory of Ronen advising Yinon to dump me, advice that had been followed after only a few months.

"And what are you doing here?" she asked with interest.

"I had an exhausting night of interrogations, so I decided to treat myself."

"Nice," she said and I had a feeling that she was a little disappointed. Since I had become a cop, anyone who ran into me seemed to fantasize that he was encountering me in the midst of a stakeout.

Her cell phone buzzed and she signaled me to wait for a minute. She peeked at the text message and it was obvious she was annoyed.

"I don't believe it!" she muttered to herself.

"What happened?" I was curious.

"The friend who was supposed to meet me here for

breakfast can't make it after all."

"Bummer."

"Yes... I took a vacation day especially for this."

"For eating breakfast here?"

"No," she smiled, "it was just the beginning of a nice day out. We planned to go shopping and go to the spa afterward."

"Can't she join you later?"

"I hope so."

"Excellent..." I answered and noticed that she was looking at the chair next to me.

"Are you eating alone?"

"Yes." I understood what she was driving at. I actually felt like eating quietly and reading a good book – a fantasy that was not about to be realized. I never understood the obsession for eating with company. Why do people need other people to eat in a restaurant? I, for instance, almost always ate my lunch alone. My coworkers at the police station had stopped asking me to join them.

Revital continued to look at me expectantly. "If you want, we could eat together," she said finally.

"Sure," I said, trying to sound welcoming. The only advantage of a joint breakfast with Revital I could think of was the option of hearing about Yinon. I imagined that she and Ronen were still in touch with my ex. "I won't let you eat alone on your birthday!"

"Excellent," she smiled and asked the waitress to bring her order to my table. After several minutes of small talk on cafés in Tel-Aviv, our food was served.

"Wow," Revital said with excitement as the waitress put the plates on the table, "a real treat."

"Yes... looks good," I said, and remembered Koby again.

"Do you eat here a lot? It seems like their lunch dishes aren't bad."

"It's my first time here."

"Did you read the recommendation in the YNET food section? There was a very flattering report on the place a week ago, so we decided to eat here. I thought you might have read it, too, and decided to give it a try."

"No... I didn't read it."

"So why did you come here?"

"Someone I work with recommended it to me," I said and immediately corrected myself, "that is, someone I worked with."

"What, the police are laying off people, too?"

"No, he died," I said and lowered my eyes.

"I'm sorry," she said in a comforting tone.

"Thank you."

"Natural causes or something else...?" she inquired.

"I'd prefer not to talk about it," I said in a choked voice.

"Okay, sorry," she bit into a fresh roll and continued with a full mouth. "So how is life as a policewoman? Last time we met, you were just starting out." She tried to calculate in her mind how much time had passed. "Wow, it's been really a long time. To the best of my memory, I was pregnant then with Guy, and he's two, now."

"It's nice."

"Just nice?"

"It's not a conventional job, but it has negative and positive aspects, like any other job. I don't have exciting experiences each day, if that's what you think. Most of the time, I do office work."

"But there's office work and there's office work..." She smiled knowingly. I knew that smile; too many people smiled like that at me. I had done what few people dared to do: I had left the golden cage in order to realize my dream. I had decided to do the work most suitable for me, not the work my bank manager judged most suitable. I was lying to Revital slightly when I said that there were negative and positive aspects; it was almost all positive. I loved being a policewoman. I loved the assignments, the structure and the people, something that, regrettably, most of my acquaintances could not say about their own work. I had learned that people do not generally appreciate hearing how much fun someone else has at work. When they hear it, they immediately try to find something negative to say about it. So, right from the start, I pretended to Revital that not everything had been perfect for me.

"Believe me, it's a job like all other jobs."

"If you say so…" she said and chewed with an open mouth.

"So how *are* Ronen and the kids?"

"Alright," she said and hurried to swallow the food remnants in her mouth. "Ronen moved to O-D-Nautika. Have you heard of it?"

"No."

"It's a gigantic international outfit. He's very well placed there."

"Very nice."

"Thanks to Yinon, to a great extent," she blurted out and was immediately embarrassed. I was actually glad she was the first one to bring up his name.

"Yinon works there, too?" I asked, making it clear how distant my contact with the man who had been my husband actually was.

"No," she said and I saw that my question surprised her. "Yinon knew someone there."

She halted her flow of words. I noticed she was

uncomfortable, but her curiosity overpowered her embarrassment.

"Aren't you in touch with Yinon?"

"No."

"Wow, I'm really sorry."

"Yes, me, too, but we realized it was the right thing for both of us to do. Didn't he tell you that?"

"When we meet up, Ronen mainly talks with him and I talk with Orit."

"With who?"

She looked at me, startled. "You don't know who Orit is?"

"No," I said, though I had already managed to figure it out by myself.

"How long since you two were last in touch?"

I took a deep breath and tried to recall our last conversation. "I think… over a year-and-a-half."

"You're not serious!" she restrained herself from shouting.

"Regrettably, yes." In fact, it was longer than that since we had seen each other. Since each encounter between us had ended between the sheets - once Yinon had realized that, even with all the love between us, I was unwilling to change my position about having a family and we both decided to avert false hopes and agony - the best things for us was to break off any contact altogether. He left me Tsumi, a sweet and spoiled dog, and got out of my life.

"So it's been quite a while since you last spoke?"

"Indeed."

"No emails or text messages?"

"Not even that."

"Surely you've seen his Facebook page."

"I don't have Facebook, and I'm quite certain he

doesn't have an account, either."

"You two are just weird!"

I laughed. It was a little sad, but her astonishment made me laugh. She joined in my laughter and, when we calmed down, I asked, "So, who's Orit?"

"You've probably guessed already... she's Yinon's partner."

"Yes."

"They met at the Sports Club. She's a Pilates instructor."

"Yinon's doing Pilates?" This was a particularly earthshaking piece of news.

"Yes. He had a very severe hip inflammation, and the doctor recommended that he took classes."

"What's she like?"

"She's a very, very sweet girl," Revital said sincerely. "Very attached to Yinon, very admiring."

"How old is she?"

"I remember we celebrated her birthday two months ago... she was twenty-eight, if I remember correctly."

"Eight years younger than him," I pointed out.

"Believe me, she's the responsible adult of the two." Revital winked at me.

My look made it clear that I did not find the joke particularly funny. When Yinon and I were married, I always felt that he was the adult between us, and not only because he was born eleven months before me.

Revital was quick to correct the overtly good impression she had created of Orit. "Overall, she's a good girl," she said and bit her lip for a moment. "But, you know, not the sharpest pencil in the box, as they say." She winked again.

This time, I smiled, mainly because I appreciated Revital's attempt to make me feel good.

"What does she look like?"

Revital swayed her head lightly as if trying to select her words. This pause made it clear that Yinon had replaced me with a younger, more athletic version, and probably a very pretty one. But Revital's answer surprised me.

"You know, female Pilates instructors are expected to be stunning…"

"I wouldn't know… I don't have too many expectations of female Pilates instructors," I answered with a smile.

"Well, whatever, of all the Pilates instructors I've ever met, Orit's the only one I'd characterize as nice. No more than that. She has - that is, she had - an amazing body, like all female Pilates instructors I know -"

"What do you mean - she had?" I cut her off. The story was starting to sound odd.

"I didn't mean to let it slip out like that," Revital lowered her eyes. "Especially since I know this subject's very charged for you… But you'll hear about it sometime anyway, so I may as well say it: Orit's expecting a baby soon."

Even though I was sitting, I had a severe sensation of dizziness. I closed and opened my eyes again and again until Revital asked if everything was okay with me.

"I need to go wash my face," I said and fled to the bathroom.

I washed my face and leaned against the sink. I stared into the mirror and it seemed to me that I was looking at a stranger. I could not decipher the jumble of emotions which engulfed me. Since Yinon and I had decided to cut off any contact between us completely - unless one of us were to change his or her position regarding bringing children into the world - I had not had a romantic relationship with any man. Here and there, someone had tried to introduce me to a guy, but I simply was not into it. Deep inside, I probably hoped that Yinon would capitulate and come back. Outwardly, I claimed that I was busy and needed peace and quiet, which was also true. I had believed - or hoped - that Yinon had been abstaining as well, and had remained faithful to me. But now I knew that, not only had he met someone new and had sex with her, but he was also about to start a family with her. Yinon had moved on and I had stayed stuck in the same place.

The tears flowed down on my cheeks uncontrollably.

The last thing I wanted was for Yinon to know that I was upset about it. It was clear that he was going to receive a complete and detailed report about the meeting. I wiped my nose and washed my face again. I returned to the table and, without sitting down, I took out my purse and left some money to cover my portion of the bill.

"I hope that's enough," I said.

"I'm sure it's fine," Revital said without looking at the money at all. She was busy watching me carefully.

"I must get to the police station," I lied, although it was clear that she realized I was lying. "Tell Yinon and Orit *Mazal Tov*," I lied again. I did not want her to tell them anything. I would have preferred that she did not even tell them we had met – but I knew there was no chance of that.

"Yes, sure," she said and I rushed to get out of there.

CHAPTER 5

As soon as I got in my car, I burst into uncontrolled sobbing again. Revital's probing glances were not holding me back anymore and I let myself release the pain. After long minutes, my outburst gradually calmed down and changed to heavy breathing. Thoughts were spinning in my mind at a dizzying rate. I tried to understand my outburst of emotions. Why did Yinon's romantic relationship, and especially his partner's pregnancy, stir me up so much? After all, I had elected to give up our relationship in order not to become a mother. Yinon loved me; I had no doubt about it! It was the reason we had decided to cut off our contact altogether. Was I regretting it now? And, like in all great tragedies, was I regretting it now when

it was already too late? I tried to isolate my sadness and my jealousy of Yinon and Orit, and asked myself if I still adhered to the principle of childlessness, but it was difficult to concentrate. The jealousy and the disappointment were stronger than me in those moments.

The phone rang and cut off the jumble of my thoughts. It was Riki from the station. I had asked her to update me when she knew the time of Koby's funeral. It turned out that the body had been released by forensics last night and the family was going to hold the funeral that day at noon, at the Yarkon Cemetery. I needed this conversation; it brought me back to reality and put my life back in perspective.

Three hours later, I was waiting with a handful of people and quite a few cops in the assembly area at the cemetery. It was the third funeral of a major criminal I had attended, and the most unlike the others. I felt confused. In the previous funerals, I had felt detached, due to my job, but this time the grief and sense of belonging immobilized me. I stood next to three cops who were engaged in an exasperating argument about a soccer game. Apparently, they were expecting many criminals to come to pay their respects to the "family member" who had passed away. But they were proven wrong. For the first time, the number of cops was identical, and perhaps even greater than the number of mourners. No criminal wanted to tie his name to an informer, even after his death.

I watched the family members starting to congregate. Koby had seven brothers and sisters, a large family by any measure, but I knew not all of them would attend. Two of his brothers lived in Los Angeles, and two more, a brother and a sister a little older than him, had shunned him after he was incarcerated for the second time. A slim, middle-aged woman was sitting on one of the benches, crying. Her crying was heart-rending. A pretty young woman was sitting next to her, holding her in a comforting hug. I assumed she was Koby's mother, who had been forced to experience the worst of all. A man I assumed was his father was sitting on her other side. He was sitting with his hands crossed and his body moving forward and backward in small motions. His eyes were red from crying. His face was deeply wrinkled, and he looked like he had not slept in two days. A small group of people congregated around Koby's parents. There was an additional young woman crying in the arms of a guy who looked her age. The rest of the people did not look like they were particularly grieved; they stood around the bereaved parents and awaited the body's arrival.

I approached Koby's mother and stood in front of her.

"Mrs. Ozri," I said in a trembling voice, "I share in your sorrow."

She raised her tearful eyes and nodded to acknowledge her gratitude. Koby's father looked straight at me and asked: "Who are you?"

"I am Hadas Levinger of the Israel Police."

"Did you know our Koby?"

"Yes," I answered with a little hesitation. I knew it would not be simple, but I felt a need to offer my condolences.

My presence aroused the curiosity of the other people and they started to gather round.

"So is it true that Koby actually worked for the police?" inquired the young woman who was hugging the young guy.

Everybody was curious. The fact that Koby was a police informer had not yet been officially confirmed.

"I can't provide you with details about an open case under investigation; I'll only tell you that, although Koby was a convicted criminal, I personally knew a different side of him. He was a very special person and I'm very sad to be here today."

Koby's mother stood up and hugged me warmly. I had to bend a little because she was shorter than me and wanted to kiss me on the cheek. Her face was wet with tears and perspiration. I felt my own cheeks growing sticky from her moistness, but knew it would be offensive to wipe my cheeks in front of her. She interlocked her arm in my arm and introduced me to her husband, who immediately burst into subdued sobbing. The pretty young woman sitting with them was Koby's youngest sister. Koby had told me about her. She was the only sibling who had kept in contact with him continuously over the years. Two additional brothers introduced themselves and their wives, and then Koby's body arrived and everybody's attention turned to the ceremony.

Koby's father delivered a short eulogy. He spoke about the well-mannered and kind-hearted Koby I had known. When he had finished, he asked if there was someone else who wanted to say something. After a pause, the firstborn son of the Ozri family approached his father. I noticed now that his eyes were also red from crying.

"Yes, Father," he said. "I want to say something."

He bent over Koby's coffin and took a deep breath. "Koby," he said in a trembling voice, "my little brother." He burst into tears and the rest of the mourners joined him. "I want to ask you for forgiveness... forgiveness for years of alienation and lack of concern. You turned to paths that were unacceptable to us, and rather than trying to help you, each of us chose to look after his own interests. We should have tried to accept you; that way, perhaps, we could have saved you. You were a good person, I always knew it. You had a bigger heart than most people I know. Forgive me, dear brother." He burst into tears again. "Forgive me."

The attendees, including some of the cops, approached him and hugged him warmly. Nobody in the congregation managed to hold back their tears.

The father's voice broke off time after time while he said the *Kaddish*. When he had finished, the funeral procession started. After all the prayers had been said and the body was lowered into the grave, the Jewish Burial Society workers tore the lapels of the family members' clothes.

"Are there any additional mourners?" a worker asked Koby's brother.

"No. We're seven siblings. Two didn't come, and two live in the United States."

"No wife or children?"

"He was divorced -" his brother started saying, and before he managed to complete his sentence, a woman and a young girl burst forth from behind.

"This is his daughter, she's also a mourner," said the woman.

I looked at them with curiosity. Koby had shown me several pictures of his ex-wife and daughter, but they were old and out of date. His ex-wife was a very good-looking woman. I knew from her pictures that she was pretty, but they did not manage to mirror the warmth and tranquility conveyed by her blue eyes. Her long hair was bundled under a black kerchief, and she was dressed simply. I knew that her life had not been easy, and that she preferred to stay away from the high life Koby had been able to offer her and their daughter.

"Daphna'leh," said Koby's mother with excitement and stretched her arms toward the girl.

Daphna, Koby's daughter, approached her grandmother and hugged her warmly. She was tall and beautiful. She had inherited her mother's hypnotizing blue eyes, and they seemed to glow in her tanned face. The grandmother and granddaughter united in a long embrace. Then one of the aunts made a tear in the lapel of Daphna's blouse, and they joined the line of mourners. They listened to the instructions about the Jewish mourning laws that applied to them and the rest of the mourners during the coming week.

I looked at the fresh grave with sadness, said my last goodbye to Koby and turned to leave.

A young voice stopped me. "Excuse me, miss…"

I turned back. It was Daphna.

"Hadas," I smiled at her. "My name is Hadas."

"Hadas." Daphna smiled and I suddenly noticed the strong resemblance between her and Koby. It was heart wrenching.

"I heard what you said… earlier," she said.

"Really? I didn't see you."

"We were standing in the back."

"I understand you're Daphna, Koby's daughter, God rest his soul."

"Correct."

I turned to Daphna's mother. "And you're his ex-wife?"

"Yes. Tali Gold." She extended her hand in greeting.

"It's nice to meet you."

"Hadas," Tali spoke in a quiet voice, "we'd like to speak with you in a more private place. Can you spare us half an hour, maybe an hour?"

"Yes, of course. Come to my office at the station; I'm on my way there now. Did you get here by car?"

"No, we came by bus."

"So come with me."

Daphna sat in the back seat and Tali took the seat next to me. After fastening her seatbelt, she untied the black kerchief on her head and loosened her hair. I noticed white strands running through her splendid mane of thick, dark hair. This woman sitting next to me did not spend her time in beauty salons. She raised her hands and shook her hair out a little. Her hands were rough and calloused. I stared at them as though she was a freak show in the circus; her somewhat masculine hands did not fit her delicate and fragile looks. It was as if another person's hands had been implanted on her.

"You have a green light." She woke me up. I continued driving, careful not to look at her or at her hands.

When we arrived at the station, I was happy to find out that Alon had already left. I knew that the conversation with Tali and Daphna was not really necessary for continuing the investigation, but Alon himself had told me more than once that too much information was preferable to too little. The colleague with whom I shared my office was out on an investigation, as usual, so we could sit down and talk undisturbed.

"Do you want anything to drink?" I asked before closing the door.

"No, thank you," they answered together.

"So. What did you want to talk to me about?" I asked, sitting across from them.

"I wanted to know if what was reported in the paper was true." Tali looked straight at me. "Was Koby a police informer?"

I smiled at her. "You don't expect me to expose the details of a confidential investigation, right?"

She inhaled deeply and said, "At the cemetery, I had the feeling that the newspaper report was true, and that you were Koby's operator. That was why you came to the funeral and approached the family like that."

"Since you're not familiar with the world of crime,

you probably don't know that there'll always be a police presence at the funerals of convicted felons, especially those with numerous convictions, or whose death occurred due to criminals settling accounts with each other. And, contrary to what people believe, we cops have a heart as well –"

"To my great regret," she cut me off and laid her hand on her daughter's knees, "I am actually familiar with the world of crime. It was a brief acquaintance, imposed on me because I chose to believe Koby when we got married. I'm almost positive I've been to this station before at least once. I never told anyone about it. Not even Daphna." She looked at her daughter lovingly and continued. "I was brought in for questioning while I was still married to Koby."

My curiosity was piqued. "Do you remember in connection with what?" I checked carefully.

"Not really, mostly because I really didn't have a clue what he was up to. When I met him, I was very young, just graduated from high school. I was mature for my age, but definitely young and inexperienced. My parents warned me against him. They knew he had a criminal record and begged me to stay away from him, but the love between us was too strong, and I believed he'd leave the world of crime for my sake." Tali began to cry. Daphna bent over toward her and hugged her warmly.

"I don't regret what I did. I loved Koby," continued Tali. She turned her flushed face toward her daughter and said in a voice that astonished me with its calmness: "I never stopped loving your father. But you know I wasn't willing to live with his lifestyle." Daphna responded with a loving smile. "On principle, I always make an effort not to regret what I've done in my life, especially not in this case, when the prize I received is so amazing." She pointed her finger at Daphna, who blushed a little in response. "It should be said, to Koby's credit, that he tried, all those years, to be a part of our lives. I didn't let him, not because I hated him, but because I loved him. I was always worried about him, and it turned out it was for a reason." She started crying again.

Daphna asked, "Shall I get you some water?"

"No, my sweetie, it's alright," she said and continued. "I wanted to live an honest, simple life. I don't need a luxury car, designer clothes or servants. I wanted to sleep well at night and he couldn't give me that. My only condition for us to be a family was for him to stay away from crime. Unfortunately, this condition was too difficult for him. The more Daphna grew up, the harder it became for me. I was afraid for her life when she was with him and I was also concerned about her education. I admit those were the reasons I did everything to keep them apart." She looked at her daughter sadly. "I apologize, my sweet. Perhaps I shouldn't have kept you away from your father like that; I felt I had to do it to protect you."

"It's alright, Mother," whispered Daphna, "I'm not angry."

"In any case," Tali turned to look at me, "what I'm trying to tell you here is that I want to know if I was wrong all those years... if I was wrong to keep Daphna away from her father because I thought he was a criminal, while, in fact, he may have been a policeman, or at least working with the police. This is what I want to know. I want to make amends. I owe it to myself, to my daughter, and mainly to Koby."

She fell silent. I waited for her to continue talking, but she only stared at me with her huge blue eyes.

I thought about Koby, about how much he had loved the woman and the girl who were now sitting opposite me. He would have given everything to turn back the clock and make different choices in his life. His daughter had been the only truly important thing for him. I knew they deserved it, and he, too – his memory – deserved that I volunteer some information.

"I can tell you one thing. In all the years I've been a policewoman - okay, maybe not all that long - but, according to what I know, for many years before me, there was no one else who helped the police in the fight against organized crime like Koby Ozri."

This dramatic statement opened up Daphna's floodgate. Now both of them were sitting across from me, sobbing excitedly and hugging each other.

"Can you give any details?" asked Tali.

"Regrettably, no. I've already said too much and I strongly ask you to keep it between us. The investigation's still going on. I said what I said because of the great admiration I felt for Koby, and because I know how much he loved the two of you and how much the separation from you had hurt him."

"I'm so sorry," sobbed Tali, caressing Daphna's shoulder.

"You don't have to be sorry. Many family members prefer to cut themselves off from someone who's turned to crime. Koby understood that. It hurt him, but he understood. In many instances, he himself kept his distance from you to keep you out of harm's way. I don't want to reveal too many details, but Koby wasn't a police informer all his life. He was an active criminal. He crossed the lines only in the last few years. Your choice was justified. On the other hand, I can tell you, to allow you to mourn him with love, that the good he did over the last few years exceeded the bad ten times over."

"It's amazing." Tali smiled a bitter smile. "When I married him, I knew about his criminal record, but also saw his good side. I'm so glad that the good in him won over the bad in the end."

"But why didn't he come to us and tell us that he was, in fact, working with the police?" asked Daphna in a sad voice. "We could have enjoyed the last few years with him, at least."

"But, that way, his identity would have been exposed," I explained.

"It was exposed anyway," Tali sighed.

CHAPTER 6

Thursday, June 16, 2011

The house of Moshe and Ilana Navon stood in the middle of a pastoral neighborhood in Hod Hasharon, an old-fashioned area of family homes, a sort of a village within a city. The buildings were not ostentatious or contemporary in style, but old, surrounded by well-cultivated gardens and crisscrossed by clean streets. It was the Israeli suburban dream.

I arrived in the late morning, so as not to run into a crowd of mourners. A large obituary notice with Shirley's name on it covered the gate. I pushed it lightly and entered. The Navon family garden, like all the gardens in the neighborhood, was beautifully cultivated. A brick path divided the garden in two, leading from the gate to the entrance to the house; two large olive trees on the right were flanked by several herb bushes. On the other side was a garden table, four matching chairs and barbeque area. I imagined the Navon family celebrating Independence Day in the garden just a few weeks earlier. They had probably argued about politics or about the elimination of Osama Bin Laden. Now, all the arguments and all the stories would remain as dim memories of another life gone forever.

Another obituary notice hung on the door. I peeked at it to see who the official family mourners were: parents and one brother. The door of the house was not open as is customary during a *shiva*, probably because of the heat outside. It was very hot. I knocked on the door lightly. Several seconds later, the door opened.

"Shalom," said a tall, attractive young man. He spoke in a quiet voice and signaled me to enter. I nodded silently and entered the foyer.

As I expected, the living room was not crowded with mourners. Moshe Navon was sitting on the sofa, leafing through a photo album. His eyes were red. Two young women were sitting on the other side of the room and talking in a whisper.

"Did you come for Yoni?" asked the young man and looked at me with interest.

"Yoni?"

"Shirley's fiancé."

"Ah." I smiled an embarrassed smile. "No. I'm Hadas Levinger from the Israel Police." I extended my hand to him.

"Nice to meet you," he said solemnly, "I'm Ido, Shirley's brother. I didn't recognize you, so I assumed you were from Yoni and Shirley's circle of friends."

"First of all, I want to express my own sincere condolences for your terrible loss, and also on behalf of the Israel Police."

"Thank you," he said. I noticed how his eyes, which had been dry, suddenly filled up with tears. I had noticed that whenever I expressed my sorrow in the name of the State, it stirred up strong emotions. I found it difficult to understand. I had never gotten too excited during the ceremonies for Holocaust Memorial Day, or the

Memorial Day for the fallen soldiers of Israel's wars, while people around me were emotionally drained. It was interesting. Was it something about the formality of it that evoked emotion in most people?

"May I speak to your parents?"

"Yes, sure." He wiped his wet eyes with his hand and signaled me to follow him into the living room.

"Dad," he stood by his father, who was still immersed in the photo album, "there's someone from the police here."

Moshe broke away from the album and looked at me through red eyes. He did not need my condolences in the name of the Police and the State in order to shed tears. He rose slowly from the sofa and walked away without saying a word to me. A few moments later he returned to the living room accompanied by a short woman, his wife, Ilana. It appeared that the mourning had made her even smaller. Ilana stood despondently by Moshe, looking like she had not slept for long days. Two pairs of red eyes looked at me and awaited my statement. It was not the first time I had faced people who had lost someone most dear to them. However, this time it was especially difficult for me. I felt I was in mourning as well. Perhaps it was actually a sense of guilt. Had I not activated Koby, he would not have been eliminated, and Shirley would not have become an unfortunate victim.

"I share in your sorrow," I said, almost in a whisper. The official version slipped my memory.

"Thank you," said Ilana softly. It was apparent that her husband was making a great effort not to burst out at me. "Do you want to sit down?"

"Yes, if possible. Perhaps we could talk in a more private place?"

"Certainly." She led us to another of the rooms inside

the house.

"It's important for me to clarify," I said right after we sat down in a room serving as a guest bedroom, "that my visit is a regular, mandatory procedure. Since you're sitting *shiva*, I've come to your home. However, I must question you, since your daughter was a fatality in a criminal incident. At present, we've no reason to suspect that your daughter was connected to the reason for it. In our estimation, she happened to be at the crime scene by accident —"

"I really want to understand!" Moshe could not restrain himself any longer. He spoke angrily. "How can innocent citizens walk safely in the streets when these crime gangs behave as if there's no law and no justice? We live in a country with enough security issues. We'll eventually get to a state when we simply won't be able to leave the house. I -"

Ilana cut him off. "Moshe," she spoke to him in the same soft tone, "You're right, but this nice policewoman isn't responsible for all the country's problems. She came here to do her job. Let her talk."

Moshe breathed heavily. The tears of sorrow were now just a glint in his eyes.

"I've no way to describe how sorry I am for your loss," I continued. "Believe it or not, I think exactly like you. I wish we could do more. In order to bring the murderer to justice, we must catch him first. Unfortunately, cases like these involve highly professional people; it's very hard to catch them. However, when they're caught, they're generally put away for a long time."

"And what about the people who send them?" asked Ilana.

"This is a lot harder to prove, but here, too,

sometimes we manage to get to the most senior individuals."

"So. What do you want to ask us?" asked Moshe impatiently.

"As I said, we have to question you. I truly hope it won't be necessary to bother you to come to the station at the end of the *shiva*. I'll only ask you about Shirley, and I apologize in advance if they upset you. It's a necessary part of the procedure in a murder investigation."

They nodded and I continued. "Tell me a little about Shirley."

"Shirley was an amazing young woman," Ilana burst into a monolog. "She's our second child, she has an older brother, Ido - you met him at the door. She was always a beautiful, smart girl. She was an Infantry instructor in the Army, commanded scores of men, and it was there that she met Yoni Shapira, who became her fiancé. She was supposed to receive a certificate of merit from the president on Independence Day, but she was discharged a month before Independence Day, and they gave the certificate to someone else."

"Well done," I said. "When was she discharged?"

"A little over four years ago. After the Army, she traveled with Yoni to South America for a year. When they returned, they registered for their academic studies. They were both about to finish their third year, Yoni in medicine and she in economics and accounting."

"She was a student?"

"You sound surprised," Moshe said in an offended tone of voice.

"Not surprised, but I was wondering about it as there's no campus near the scene of the incident, and, to our understanding, she had arrived at the scene to pick up her lunch."

"Shirley attended Tel-Aviv University," explained Ilana. "The course she chose included an option for taking summer semesters, so she simply took courses earlier and progressed faster. She was well organized; she wanted to be hired by one of the most prestigious accounting firms in the country next year, and it was important to her to start work ahead of time, so she could demonstrate experience in bookkeeping. She'd been told that the public accountants in the large firms don't have sufficient knowledge in bookkeeping."

"She was on the Dean's list in the first two years, even though she crammed her schedule with more courses than any other student in those years," added Moshe with pride. Ilana nodded in agreement.

"We're very proud of her," she said and wiped her nose. "In any case, this year she had a lot more time for working and also for studying. She and Yoni got engaged and moved in together, and it was another incentive for her to work. Less than a year ago, I think, she started bookkeeping for Panda."

"The cellular company?"

"Yes, they're not far from the place where the murder took place."

"I know," I said. It was impossible to miss the huge sign of the country's largest cellular company. "What did she tell you about her work?"

"Not too much," said Ilana.

"I think she was very satisfied there, and they were also very satisfied with her," added Moshe immediately.

"You exaggerate a little." Ilana smiled. "Moshe adored Shirley - we all adored her - and I've no doubt she was very successful in her work. But she was too busy to tell us much about it, and, in any case, we could never understand what she was talking about. I'm a Literature teacher and Moshe has a carpentry shop, so our only connection to the financial world are the tax receipts we hand over each month to Moshe's accountant."

"What can you tell me about her fiancé?"

"Yoni?" Ilana asked, as if her daughter had been engaged to several men.

"Yes, Yoni."

"Yoni was an officer at the military base where she served. He gave her a ride home one day and the rest was history."

"You said he was studying medicine?"

"Right."

"Does he work as well?"

"Only on his vacations," said Ilana. "It's very hard to combine work with medical studies."

"Can you please write down his phone number for me?" I asked gently and extended a piece of paper and a pen to her.

"Excuse me," Moshe interfered and turned to me. "Why does this interest you? Why do you have to know where Yoni's studying and what he's doing? Why do you want to speak with him?"

"Moshe," Ilana tried to mollify him, "she's only doing her job."

"Right. You have to understand that your daughter was a victim of a serious criminal incident. I have only one goal here: to learn about the victim."

"But to my unprofessional ear, it seems as if the police are looking for the murderer in our family, when any idiot can understand that it was a mafia hit! Why do you care at all what Shirley and Yoni studied, or where they worked? How will that advance the investigation? At this moment, the murderer who took my daughter's life is walking around free in the State of Israel. I can guarantee it's not Yoni, and it has no connection to him whatsoever! Yoni's no less than the salt of the earth. An outstanding officer and medical student. A man who just lost the woman he loved, the one who was supposed to be the mother of his children."

Ilana burst into tears and Moshe bent over to hug her.

I was silent. What could I say?

I knew already that I would not be able to fill in the form with the victim's details, at least not at that stage.

Moshe and Ilana broke away from their embrace.

"I can't stop thinking about it," Ilana said in a choked voice. "I won't have grandchildren from my beautiful girl…"

"Did Shirley want to have children?" I asked.

"Obviously," said Moshe tightly. "Is there anyone who doesn't want to have kids?"

I did not answer.

"We wanted to have many children," Ilana continued, "but fate brought us only two. Once, someone who could not have kids simply did not have them, unlike today, when there's treatment available. I was longing to have grandchildren, to hold a little soft body again, to hear the sound of rolling laughter and chase after a sweet toddler all over the house. My brother has three grandchildren already, my sister has two, and Moshe's sister has four grandchildren! I thought my turn had finally come…" She rolled her eyes and covered her mouth with her hand, as if trying to prevent sobs from bursting out again.

"You'll have grandchildren from your son," I tried to console them.

"Ah," she moaned, "my son doesn't intend to settle down anytime soon."

I sat with them a little longer. They showed me

Shirley's certificates of merit and pictures from different periods in her life. I left their house with the feeling that I had contributed nothing to the investigation, but at least I had consoled two bereaved parents.

CHAPTER 7

Nobody at the police station bothered to bring me up to date about Alon's particularly combative mood. I gave him an overly cheery, "Hello!" only to receive a downpour of yelling and swearing in return. He screamed that he had no idea where I had been wandering off to, and asked why he was not receiving enough reports, and how it could be that there had been no progress in my cases. He went on screaming that he had passed by my office and had been shocked by the amount of paperwork on my desk. I wanted to tell him that I had been working an average of twelve hours a day and doing the work of at least two cops. However, I knew that when Alon was in such a state - probably as a direct result of a conversation with his ex-wife - the last thing to do was to answer him. I dragged myself, "full of motivation," to my room, to discover that no paperwork fairy had arrived and cleared the piles of documents waiting for me. I had immersed myself in reading the scores of interrogation reports that had been piling up on my desk over the last few days, when my cell buzzed. I answered.

"You dare not shirk it again," my sister's voice declared jubilantly.

"Shirk what?"

"You're not serious?" Shira almost yelled. "No, you're simply unreal."

"What?" I asked impatiently. "Shira, I really have no patience for a quiz… I've no idea what you want from me."

"You promised you'd join us this time and not find a last-minute excuse!"

"Ah, the *vaibers*…" Once every few weeks, the *vaibers* (Yiddish for "wives") - my mother, her sister Nira and their daughters, that is my sisters, Shira and Ayala and my cousin, Orly - would meet for a light dinner in a pleasant café in Givat Shmuel, to gossip and catch up. Since I had no kids and since most of the discussion revolved around stories about grandchildren, those get-togethers were a pain in the neck for me. During the last one I attended (I had failed to find a timely excuse) we were sitting on such a comfortable sofa that I simply fell asleep.

"The café in Givat Shmuel. Half an hour."

"I completely forgot about it."

"So here I am, reminding you."

"I'll never get there in half an hour. I'm still at the station."

"Then leave right now. At the most, you'll be ten minutes late. Ayala will be late for sure."

"Fine…" I answered in a low voice. The truth was that my level of concentration was close to zero, and I thought that after three such loaded days, a little familial support would not hurt me.

Three quarters of an hour later, the women of the family embraced me affectionately. Since, over the last few months, I had usually missed family get-togethers, I was the guest of honor.

"Either we don't see you at all, or I see you twice in the same week," said my aunt and laughed aloud.

"When did we see each other this week?" I asked, surprised, and sat down next to Shira.

Ayala joined in the laughter. "Wow, what a space cadet! At the bris, of course… Evyatar and Efrat's son."

"Perhaps she didn't get to see you." Mother rushed to my rescue. "Right in the middle of the bris she was summoned to an incident in Tel-Aviv."

"You're both right," I smiled, embarrassed. "I did actually see you. We even chatted a little! But as mom said, I was called in by my work and the last few days have been crazy, so I got a little confused."

"You're talking about the hit that took place in the center of Tel-Aviv?" asked Orly with curiosity.

"Hmm…" I nodded, looking at the menu. How disappointing – the menu had changed completely since the last time I was there.

"What a tragedy," said my aunt in a not-to-be disputed tone of voice. "A young woman goes out to eat lunch, and a gang of criminals shoot her only because she was standing in the wrong place."

"They have no boundaries," said Ayala. "As if all the terror attacks weren't enough for us, these criminals conduct their gang wars in the middle of the street!"

"Let them kill each other in their own homes, not in our streets," added Orly.

I pretended to immerse myself in the menu. I had already heard similar comments more than once during the last week, and they were not pleasant to hear. Shirley was, indeed, an unintended and unnecessary victim of the crime war, but, for me, Koby was a close friend. I did not wish for his death, not in the heart of Tel-Aviv, nor in his private home.

The voices around the table became silent and I realized that they were waiting to hear my statement.

"It's getting on my nerves," I said and put down the menu melodramatically, "that they're always changing the menus in restaurants!"

They all laughed. I also smiled, even though I absolutely meant what I said. "I always ordered their pasta salad here. Now I've no idea what to have."

"Order the tomato and pine cone pasta," suggested Shira. "It's exactly the same."

"Then why change the name?" I raged. They laughed again. This time I did not smile. I did not understand what was funny.

"It appears to me that the one who tried to change the subject of this discussion was you," Aunt Nira teased me.

"Perhaps you'd leave her alone?" My mother defended me again. "She's not allowed to discuss her work."

She turned to me and smiled at me with understanding. I smiled back. I knew that, later on, she would try to squeeze all the juicy details of the case out of me. I tried to understand why she had been so protective of me lately. Was it that motherly instinct that everybody talked about, which seemed to have been stirred up in her lately, or was it her wish to be the first and exclusive source of all the information at my disposal?

"The truth is, I don't have too much to tell," I said and sipped my Coke.

"Fine... we won't bother you," said my aunt in a placating tone of voice. "Did you hear our news?"

"What news?"

"Orly's pregnant again!" answered my aunt jubilantly

and bestowed a warm, suffocating embrace on her daughter. Orly was two years older than me. For years, we had shared the same pitying looks reserved for childless women. I, at least, had been married for a not-too-short period, but Orly had only got married three years ago, at the advanced age of thirty-four. A year after her wedding, she gave birth to a son, and now she was about to bring another offspring into the world. Indeed, my dear aunt could leave this world without any cloud hovering above her only daughter's head.

"Congratulations!" I called out, adding in a near-whisper, "Indeed, everybody's pregnant..." I added in a whisper.

"What?" Shira heard me muttering and shrieked at once, "Who else is pregnant?"

"Yinon's wife."

"Your Yinon?!" Ayala and Shira were shocked.

"It turns out he's not really mine anymore," I said and knew that the chance of holding back my tears was nil. My mother rushed to get up and hug me. In the background, I heard my aunt asking Shira when Yinon had remarried. "I didn't know that he'd remarried at all," she answered in a whisper.

I do not cry a lot, and when it happens, I try not to do it in front of other people. It does not fit with the image I try to construct for myself. Rather, just as I find it difficult to handle other people's sorrow, it is hard for me to handle other people's reaction to my sorrow. I cannot bear the thought that I am the object of pity. However, this time around, my mother's hug was the thing I needed most. I felt like a five-year-old girl again, and Mother's protective embrace shielded me from the whole world.

"How long have you known about it?" she asked me.

"Just since yesterday."

"Why didn't you share it with me right away?"

"I didn't have the time."

She looked at me, full of compassion. I knew what she was thinking. For each phone call from me, my sisters called her about five hundred times. They called her several times a day in order to update her with trivialities, while I did not even call her to tell her about something so fundamental.

"It's not good to keep things locked up inside." She cuddled me gently. "You'll give yourself an ulcer."

"Right," I said and broke away from her embrace, which had become oppressive.

I went to the bathroom to blow my nose and wash my face. When I returned to the table, I saw Aunt Nira looking at me with that look, the one my mother had managed to wean herself from. It said, "I told you so."

"All's well!" I said in the most joyful voice I could assume.

"If you say so." My aunt could not stop herself, and my mother gave her a blood -curdling look.

"Aunt Nira," I told her calmly, "I know that all that reverberates in your head now is 'I told you so,' but I can assure you: I haven't changed my mind about parenting. I'm sad because my story with Yinon is over in a final way. That's all." I hoped I sounded convincing, because I had to convince myself as well.

We managed to finish dinner without additional scenes, to my mother's great delight. We avoided talking about anything that could cause one of us to burst into tears, which more or less limited the conversation to talking about the weather and reality shows, most of which I had never heard of.

I returned home relaxed and full. I took Tsumi out

for a walk and went to bed before eleven. I could not remember when I had settled to sleep so early in the last two months. I decided I had had enough drama for one week, and planned to spend the weekend in bed with a good book and some food, which I would get from my mother the following day. I fell asleep with a sweet smile of expectation.

My smile disappeared at 2:00 A.M., when my cell phone woke me up.

"Hello?" I half-said, half-asked sleepily.

"Hadas Levinger?" The authoritative voice at the other end also half-spoke, half-asked.

"Yes…" My sleepy voice became confused.

"This is Attorney Idan Margolin from the District Attorney's office. Are you the investigator in the murder case of Koby Ozri and Shirley Navon?" He got to the point right away.

"Right."

"Great," he breathed heavily. It was apparent from his voice that he had endured several particularly stormy hours.

"We have a state's witness for your case, it appears."

"What?" My confusion became perplexity.

"We have someone who claims that he knows who murdered Koby Ozri and Shirley Navon."

I was silent. I was shocked and speechless. He continued: "Can you get to the station now for a preliminary interrogation of the witness?"

"Fifteen minutes," I answered and parted from my bed with a sorrowful look.

CHAPTER 8

Anya Ivanov hated life in Russia. She had only been a little girl when the old Soviet regime had been in power, so she had to believe her parents when they said that life was currently a paradise compared to what it had been in the past. Still, she was a young, educated woman. She even toured Europe for a while when she was invited to do some modeling in Milan, so she knew that life in Russia was very far from what the West had to offer young people. As an only child, she found it hard to leave her loving, aging parents, but she knew that she would not want to put down roots in Moscow or in any other city in Russia. She was a beautiful young woman, tall and shapely, her long blond hair framed her pretty face, and her large, blue eyes glowed like two gemstones.

In Milan, she received quite a few job offers and several fashion designers practically begged her to stay and continue modelling for them. But she opted to return to Moscow to complete her degree in electronic engineering. Anya was determined to succeed in life. A lot of guys courted her, but she was careful not to fall in love. In reality, she did not have to be too careful; she was disgusted by the typical Russian masculine chauvinist. She longed for a man who would listen to her, and let her express herself without fear — not from him, and not from society's response.

Her beloved father had been one of the rare men she had known who had not been a chauvinist. He had treated her mother like an equal. He had never beaten her, had never sworn at her, and had always encouraged her to express her opinion fearlessly. She remembered well how her girlfriends had been shocked by her parents' conduct during her birthday party. It turned out that her father had brought the wrong cake from the confectionery.

"Dimitri!" her mother said angrily when she realized that another child's name was written on the cake in creamy letters. "It's not the cake I ordered!"

Her father apologized and rushed off to replace the cake at once.

Other mothers would have covered the cake with a layer of cream and decorated it with the correct name. None of them would have dared to send her husband to bring a new cake, and would certainly not have yelled at him in the presence of strangers.

During the difficult winter of 2009, her father was stricken with severe flu and infected her mother. They were old and sick and both of them passed away within three months. After recovering from her deep mourning, Anya knew that nothing was holding her in Russia any more. She started looking for work in various countries in Europe, and tried her luck in the US and Canada as well. But the world had been steeped in its own mourning and had not recovered yet from severe economic instability. Unemployment was rife everywhere in the world, and good jobs were snapped up fast. Anya's prospects of getting a position — as a foreigner who did not speak the language well — were low.

She completed her internship in engineering, but, without good connections, she was out of the loop as far as good positions were concerned. And she did not have connections. In the end, she was accepted for a position that even a high school graduate could do with her eyes closed and her hands tied. At a certain point, she considered going back to modeling. She was now twenty-eight, a young woman by any measure, but in the realm of modeling, she was considered to be a dinosaur. Her few girlfriends and male friends were in various stages of romantic relationships and one girlfriend was even pregnant, and Anya began to feel stuck. There were still quite a few guys interested in her, though fewer than before, but she still insisted that she was not interested in Russian men. Once in a while, she relented and dated someone, only to discover that she should have trusted her instincts after all.

About six months after her parents' passing, Anya decided to try her luck with international dating websites. She had done some research on the subject and knew of several websites where Western men advertised for Russian brides. However, there were also some websites where it was possible to meet men who were interested in an egalitarian relationship. She registered with one of those, along with men and women from all over the world, and felt safe. Her profile was rather attractive; she was young and good-looking and received many responses. The main obstacle was the language. Though Anya's English was quite good, she found it hard to type fast in English, and the more difficult problem was that many guys whose profiles she liked did not know any English.

Two weeks after she had registered on that website, she already started to lose hope that she would find love there. But then she received a response from a guy named Ilan. The name intrigued her. She never heard of such a name. She examined his profile: thirty-two, and from Israel. Her late father had admired the State of Israel and used any opportunity to tell how his maternal grandfather was of Jewish origins. Her father had told her that Israel was a small state in the Middle East, and, though surrounded by hostile countries, it had a strong army and a modern economy. She also knew that quite a few Russian-speaking Jews had immigrated to Israel after the dissolution of the Soviet Union. She examined Ilan's picture. He looked robust, healthy and tanned. He looked somewhat Middle-Eastern, which intrigued her. After a correspondence of several stuttering sentences in English, Ilan asked if she would prefer to correspond in Russian. Anya was surprised. Ilan did not look like someone with Russian roots. She was, of course, glad to switch to her native language. Soon she discovered that Ilan was fluent in the language, though he wrote with quite a few errors. Ilan told her that his parents had immigrated to Israel from Odessa in 1971, right after getting married. He and his two brothers were born in Israel, and spoke Russian at home and Hebrew at school, but since he had never learned to write in Russian, he made many mistakes.

The conversations with Ilan grew longer and longer. They soon left the chatroom and switched to Skype. Ilan's spoken Russian was perfect. In their first video conversation, Anya discovered that Ilan was as handsome as his picture. He was pleasant, courteous, and had a wonderful sense of humor. His stories about Israel charmed her. He told her that he had studied software engineering and had an MBA. He had set up a start-up company with a friend, which had been sold to

Microsoft after five years for a large sum, which he preferred not to specify.

Anya was somewhat skeptical about Ilan's success stories, but after that conversation she conducted a quick search on the internet and found that, two years earlier, Microsoft had bought the company specified by Ilan for 50 million $US. She still could not be certain that Ilan was, indeed, the man he had claimed to be, but he definitely won her esteem. Ilan told her about the advanced high-tech industry in Israel and hinted that a talented engineer like her could easily find work in Israel.

"But I'm not Jewish," she laughed. "I can't immigrate to Israel."

"You could marry an Israeli," he winked.

Anya still found it difficult to understand why a young, handsome and wealthy guy like Ilan was searching for a romantic relationship on an international dating website. As a matter of fact, she realized, she could ask the same question about herself. Finally, she asked Ilan about it. She discovered that he had registered with the website for the same reason she had registered. Ilan told her that he did not like the mentality of Israeli women, and was looking for a woman from a Russian background. "Like Mama," he laughed. Anya was somewhat concerned that she might travel all the way to Israel just to discover that the man she liked so much from a distance was just the same as any typical Russian man. But the more she talked to Ilan, the more her concern diminished. Ilan was well-mannered and pleasant. Two weeks after they had started Skyping, Ilan told her he must meet her face to face and booked a flight to Moscow. Anya met him at the airport, and, as soon as she saw him, had no doubt that she was in love. She accompanied him to his hotel, the most extravagant in Moscow. Despite her instant attraction, she refrained from going with him to his room. She did not want to appear desperate. They spent an incredible weekend. Ilan behaved like a perfect gentleman and did not attempt to touch her without her consent. Three days later, she gave way to her desire and they made love.

Their parting was difficult, but the meeting made it clear to Anya that she had found the love of her life. Now she only hoped she would love Israel. Before she could even start looking for a good deal for her flight, Ilan surprised her with a business class ticket as a gift.

Her boss did not like her request for vacation at such a short notice, but Anya already knew that she would probably not return to her dull work in the warehouse, sorting and cataloging electronic components.

Indeed, she never did return to her work there.

The flight to Israel was wonderful. Though she had never flown business class and was thrilled with the various perks, she was eager to land, meet Ilan again and get to know Israel, the country which would probably become her home.

After collecting her small suitcase, she went out to the arrivals hall. Ilan was waiting for her, holding a red rose in his hand. She ran toward him and they kissed passionately. He stroked her flowing hair and told her excitedly how much he had missed her. She was floating with happiness. This euphoria changed a few minutes later when they exited the terminal building into the open air and the Israeli humidity. It was in the middle of October. In Moscow, heaters were already working at full capacity, but in Israel it was as if someone had left the heaters on outside! Anya could not believe that it could be so hot in October. Ilan smiled as he opened the door of a luxury car for her. She sat down in the front seat next to the driver, buckled her seatbelt and fell asleep right away.

When she woke up several hours later in a dark, suffocating room, she realized that she had actually arrived in Hell. She thought that she and Ilan must have been kidnapped. But as she struggled to recall what had happened before she fell asleep, she realized to her horror that Ilan was the kidnapper. From sweet euphoria, she descended into misery and bitter despair. She remembered his smile as he opened the door of a large, black car with dark windows. She had thought that, in Israel, everyone drove such cars because of the strong sun. She remembered glimpsing an additional person in the back seat and recalled seeing him pulling out a syringe, and a light sting in her arm as she buckled herself in. She remembered nothing else after that.

Having committed no crime, she was now locked up for twenty months in a prison where all the prisoners were miserable women.

She did not see Ilan again, but she saw many other men, for sure. At first, she refused to cooperate. However, to her regret, there were men who wanted her even more because of that, and scores of them raped her, sometimes several of them together. In time, she came to understand that if she wanted to survive and befriend the other girls, she would have to accept her fate. She began to talk to her fellow-sufferers and discovered that most of the girls in that "prison" (this was how she thought of the place, knowing no other details about it) were simple girls from isolated villages in Eastern Europe. Some of them had known that they were coming to Israel to work in prostitution; some had thought that they would be sold to Israeli men as brides, and others had been told that they would work as housekeepers. She was the only one who had arrived from a big city, the only one with an academic degree, a stranger among strangers. She understood that Ilan had seduced her because she had been alone and nobody would be looking for her.

The other girls did not like her. Most of them had serious orthodontic problems, while others looked older than their age, with their flabby skin and sagging breasts. She was young and beautiful, and the moment she stopped resisting, the demand for her soared and she received a more considerate attitude and more positive attention from the pimps. However, Anya was in great distress, and struggling. She did not want to make enemies. Several rowdy confrontations made it clear to her that she must find a way to win the hearts of the other girls. She understood from her few conversations with the girls that they were receiving hard drugs that dulled the pain of their existence. Most of them wanted additional fixes, but did not get them because their captors wanted them to be cheerful, not dazed. She began asking for drugs herself and distributed her quota among the women she identified as the leaders of the bunch. Her social position improved miraculously and she began thinking about an escape plan. She knew that she must remain lucid and wait for the right moment.

After six months of imprisonment, she was allowed out of the house as a reward for her good and obedient behavior. Alex, the loyal assistant of Itzik, the proprietor of the place, accompanied her on her first stroll in Israel. Anya decided not to use this excursion to escape, but to examine her surroundings.

She was shocked. The promotional videos she had seen before leaving Moscow had presented a very different Israel than the one she saw before her. The streets surrounding the house where she was being held were crowded, dirty and old. There were filthy beggars, drug addicts and drunks lying on the sidewalks. She had not understood why so many of the clients were dark skinned. She thought Israelis had lighter skin. Now that she was walking around outside, she saw that most of the passers-by were of African origin. Her escort took her to a hairdresser, also of African origin, to cut and style her hair. Then they walked over to a street where there were several vendor stands and Anya was allowed to buy herself new clothes and cosmetic products.

The excursion taught Anya several important things. First, she understood that the house where she was being held was in one of the poorest neighborhoods in Israel. In the hairdresser's salon, she saw drugs being bought and sold right in front of her. One thing she did not see were cops. She knew that when she did manage to escape, she would have to run far away.

After that excursion, Anya was allowed to leave a few more times, but she did not try to escape. She knew she had to wait for the appropriate opportunity, because if she failed, she would not get another chance.

The right opportunity arrived after twenty months and hundreds of men. One morning, a few hours before the beginning of "working hours," black smoke penetrated the apartment and spread through the rooms. The girls woke up in panic and started to run in every direction. They were locked in their living quarters because the door separating their rooms from the area where they received the clients was locked, as usual. Anya knew that the moment she was waiting for had arrived. She put on the running shoes she had prepared in advance, put several items in a small bag, and waited by the door for the firefighters to arrive. The smoke in the apartment became thicker, the girls became hysterical and were crying, but there was no sound on the other side of the door. Not the siren of the Fire and Rescue truck, nor the voices of the pimps. They were abandoned to their fate. Hysteria and panic took over. Katya, one of the older women, fainted; others banged on the locked door with all their strength. Suddenly, there were voices on the other side of the door. Anya became alert. To her regret, she identified the voices of Itzik and Alex. The door opened and the girls burst out, running, petrified – and stopped at once. Alex and Itzik pointed their guns at them and instructed them not to move. Alex shouted that there was a small fire on the floor above them and there was no cause for alarm. The girls shouted back that they could not breathe and that Katya had fainted. Alex and Itzik consulted each other and Anya knew that this was her moment. Through the clouds of smoke, she saw that the door of the apartment was open, and planned to walk over there quietly and cautiously. She started toward the door and stopped. Eera, one of the veteran women in the house, an embittered, heavy addict, was watching her with great interest. Anya knew that Eera would not hesitate to yell and point her out, because she would be rewarded with a fix. She was prepared for that. She put her finger to her mouth in a silent, quick motion, signaled Eera to keep quiet, and at the same time tossed toward her a generous packet of drugs. Eera grabbed the packet, peeked inside, smiled a toothless smile and waved her farewell.

Anya started running. She was weak from the smoke she had inhaled and from the many months of malnutrition, but she overcame her weakness and managed to get far away. When she was sure she was far enough away, she switched to moderate walking. The old, ugly houses changed into fashionable cafés and stylish houses. She no longer saw addicts lying on the sidewalks, nor any Africans. She stopped the first cop she saw and started crying.

I heard Anya's story from the policewoman who first interviewed her. Anya had no papers or money. The policewoman, who spoke Russian, verified Anya's identity. She managed to contact a distant relative of Anya's, who confirmed her story.

During the interview, Anya described the area surrounding the house where she had stayed. It was clear to the policewoman where the brothel was operating – the old Central Station of Tel-Aviv. The place was only a few hundred yards from refurbished Jaffa and the trendy, Bohemian area of South Tel-Aviv – but in reality, it was light years away from them.

The raid was quick and effective. Two hours after the special operations unit had broken into the place, all the women were transported to the station for continued treatment by the welfare authorities. The men who had been in the apartment at the time, Alex and Itzik, and four stunned customers, were arrested at once.

Anya identified Alex and Itzik immediately in the lineup, and they were transferred for interrogation on suspected trafficking in women, solicitation and drug dealing.

Itzik's police file revealed that his last name was Levayev, and that he had a rather scant criminal record. He had been arrested in the past for small property offenses, but never indicted. The reason was simple. Itzik traded in stolen property, in drugs, in women, and in information as well.

"I may know who murdered Koby Ozri and that girl

in Tel-Aviv few days ago," he announced to the interrogators before they even started the interrogation.

CHAPTER 9

I studied Itzik Levayev through the one-way mirror. He looked bored, almost sleepy. I was repelled by him. For me, he was a felon of the lowest level, one of those who commit terrible, horrific crimes but manage to avoid punishment.

I went to see the women who had been released from the apartment of horrors. Some were crying, while some were sitting and staring at the wall with a hollow gaze. One woman, quite old, was sitting on the floor, holding her knees and moving rhythmically. The Russian-speaking policewoman told me it was Eera, from Anya's story, and that she was the most heavily addicted. I felt sick at heart. The policewoman said that the psychiatrist on call had been summoned and that he would arrive shortly with a methadone supply.

I felt like entering the interrogation room, smiling at Itzik disdainfully and telling him that we would manage without his testimony; that, this time, he would pay for his actions. But I could not. I had a debt to Koby, to his family, and to Shirley's family. I had to do all I could to catch the murderer, even if it involved a deal with the devil. Furthermore, I would not be the one to cut the deal; it was a matter for the District Attorney's office. I only had to verify that such an agreement had a genuine value.

When I finally entered the interrogation room, Itzik raised his head toward me. He did not look confused or surprised, only a little tired. It was not his first interrogation, nor the first time he was about to become a witness for the state.

"Itzik Levayev?" I asked coldly.

"Correct," he answered hoarsely. "May I have some water?"

"Right away," I said. I wanted to give him a glass of gasoline. "My name's Hadas Levinger; I'm investigating the murder of Koby Ozri and Shirley Navon. I understand you claim to know who murdered them."

He looked at me, looking bored, then licked his lips and slowly swallowed his saliva. "I'm thirsty," he finally said. "I've been sitting here handcuffed to the desk for over an hour, without anyone coming in and asking me if I needed anything. I don't think the police need more headlines on the mistreatment of detainees."

The little squealer had no hesitation in threatening me. For a moment, I felt like giving him several more good reasons for the headline he wanted to issue. But it was obviously pointless. The bottom line was that he was not my detainee and I was not in charge of his interrogation on the trafficking of women. There was no point fighting with him; all I needed from him was a name.

"Someone bring water for Mr. Levayev!" I called toward the two-way mirror.

"A sealed bottle of mineral water," he added immediately, loudly.

I looked at him in surprise.

"You think I don't know you people spit into glasses of water?" He smiled a wise-ass smile.

Several minutes later, a sealed bottle of mineral water was placed before him. He opened the bottle and took a little sip, as if to emphasize to me that he was not particularly thirsty. It was important for him to prove who was running the show. I reminded myself who had the upper hand here.

"So what can you tell me about the murder of Koby and Shirley?" I asked him after he had closed the bottle.

He smiled with tight lips and said, "You surely don't expect me to answer that before I have a signed agreement from the D.A.'s office?"

I smiled back at him broadly. "In order for you to get a signed agreement from the D.A.'s office, I have to confirm that I'm interested in you as a witness."

His twitch of a smile was erased right away. "But if I tell you who the murderer is, what guarantee do I have that I'll get what I want?"

"Nobody said you have to give a full testimony now. The rules are clear to all parties. You give us a name, and in return you'll receive a reduced indictment, on condition, of course, that we can prove it was, indeed, the murderer."

"Believe me, he's the murderer." His voice abounded with confidence.

"I'm not in the business of belief; I'm in the business of evidence and proof."

"How can I convince you?"

"You won't convince me, I can promise you that. But you can tell me how you think you know who the murderer is. I'm not asking for a name or complete details. We'll have those after the agreement's signed. But - since, to the best of my knowledge, you weren't present at the murder scene, I'm curious to know how you know who the murderer is?"

"Let's just say, he's one of my regulars and I happened to hear him talking about it."

"He confessed to you about the murder?" I had not expected this.

"Shit, no! Do I look like a confessor to you?" He chuckled aloud and was very pleased with himself. "I heard him talking about something related and put two and two together."

Now it was my turn to chuckle. "You mean to tell me that you expect to have a signed agreement accepting you as a State's witness, which would give you reduced charges on the grave felony of trafficking in women, on the basis of your perception you have about the murderer?!"

He held his nerve. "I can vouch for it. This is the murderer." He resumed his confident tone. "What I heard and what I know about that person leaves no room for doubt. In any case, as you said yourself, the agreement won't be binding if it turns out he wasn't the murderer. I promise you – this is your man."

I despised this deplorable character. I wanted with all my heart to find a flaw or a loophole that would prevent me from proceeding with an agreement with him. Regrettably, however, there was considerable truth in what he said. There was no risk in accepting his testimony; if he gave me the wrong name, the agreement would be void. Besides, my intuition told me that he did, indeed, know the identity of the murderer.

"If the man you think is the murderer is in the country now, can we track him down easily?" I searched for another way out of the emerging deal.

"To the best of my knowledge, yes. He lives in Israel. I don't know how easy it'd be to track him down. He's not exactly an ordinary citizen."

"Does he know you're here?"

"How would I know?"

"Does he know you know he's the murderer?"

"I'd find that hard to believe."

I also found it hard to believe, but I left the interrogation room, called Attorney Idan Margolin, and confirmed the go-ahead for the deal.

Alon arrived at the station just as I was about to leave to fulfill my fantasy of a peaceful weekend. He signaled me to follow him to his office.

"What wonderful news!" he said and dropped into his chair, signaling me to sit. I sighed lightly and sat down, disappointed that he could not be satisfied with a short talk in the hallway.

"What's wonderful? Discovering that, here in this country, there are scum who lock up women they import from Eastern Europe like cattle?" I tried to chill up the celebratory air.

"Come on, really, Levinger, soon you'll be burning bras in the front yard of the station! You know exactly what I'm talking about." I lowered my eyes, mainly so that he would not notice the smile I was trying so hard to hide. "It's not every day we get a state's witness who can identify the killer within a week of the incident itself. I don't have to explain to you how uncommon it is."

"That's true," I muttered.

"How's our witness? Does he seem reliable to you?"

"Surprisingly, I have to admit that he does. He is, of course, the scum of the human race, if you ask me, but I believe he really does know who the murderer is."

"What did you settle with the D.A.?"

"He'll receive what he wants, but only after we prove that this was, indeed, the murderer."

"Do you have any idea how he knows?"

"He heard something from the murderer himself."

"And he's not afraid to inform on a murderer, just like that?"

"I really have no idea. He's not ready to reveal too much, only that the murderer frequented his brothel and that he knows for sure it was him."

"Interesting," he said and fell quiet. It seemed to me that he was trying to organize the information in his head. "So," he said after a long pause, just as I was starting to feel a little embarrassed by the long silence, "when can we interrogate the witness? On Sunday? Monday?"

I stared at him incredulously. Was he serious? This was not our first State's witness. Where did he get the fantasy that the deal could be signed within two days? And over the weekend? It didn't work like that. It had never worked like that.

"Margolin said it would take about two weeks," I said, making an effort to hide the tremor in my voice, knowing full well what was about to happen. And indeed, even before I had finished the sentence, Alon burst out in a rage.

"Two weeks?" he screamed. "Two weeks?!" He clasped his head with his hands as if to prevent it from exploding, something I definitely believed might happen. "Did you tell this dummy to explain to the dummies at the D.A.'s office that this is an ongoing murder investigation and the murderer could vanish by then?"

The truth was that I had not mentioned anything like that. I simply asked Idan to do all he could to expedite the process. I did not feel like letting a despicable felon like Itzik get too good a deal because of pressure from our side.

"I told him we wanted to interrogate the witness as soon as possible."

"And as far as you're concerned, two weeks is soon!?"

"He committed horrible crimes and –"

"For fuck's sake!" he interrupted me again, stuttering with impatience. "We're not the Girl Scouts, is that clear? We've seen and investigated horrible crimes; we've seen felons leaving court with certificates of good character worthy of Mother Teresa! We're in the business of closing cases... this is what we do! We've got an opportunity here to close two cases with one blow!" He turned away to find his cell phone, and I used the opportunity to roll my eyes as required. When he wanted, Alon could also deliver an hour-long speech about the fucked-up system that lets dangerous felons go free.

"Don't think I didn't see that eye rolling, Levinger," he said as he turned toward me again.

"You could be a teacher. You have eyes in the back of your head," I chuckled. He smiled.

I saw his finger stab urgently at his cell phone screen, searching out a certain phone number. He reached for the phone on his desk, picked it up and dialed.

"Who are you calling?" I asked him.

"Edna Kahana, the Deputy D.A."

"You know her?"

"I've had the opportunity to speak to her several times," he smiled. I already knew she was a woman he had somehow managed to charm with his macho personality and defective sense of humor, which only those devoid of a sense of humor would find funny.

Alon turned on the speaker.

After several rings, a sleepy female voice said, "Hello?"

"Edna!" Alon said in a confident, smiley voice.

"Who is this?" asked Edna, yawning, as was appropriate for the day (Friday) and for the hour (6:30 in the morning).

"This is Superintendent Alon Dor of the Tel-Aviv Central Unit."

"Who?"

"Alon Dor... we've met several times. The last time was at the D.A.'s fundraiser for police orphans. We sat at the same table."

"Alon!" The tone of her voice had changed at once and became cheerful, even a little coquettish. "How can I assist you?"

"First of all, I want to make it clear that you're on speaker, and that Inspector Hadas Levinger is present."

"Shalom," I said almost in a whisper.

"Shalom, Hadas." The excitement in Lady Edna's voice diminished a little.

"Edna, I don't want to disturb you too much on a Friday morning, so I'll make it brief." I did not think for a moment that Alon even knew how to talk at length. "We have a state's witness who's willing to give us the murderer in the case of Koby Ozri and that girl..."

"Shirley Navon," I added immediately.

"Yes... and Shirley."

"Wow," she exclaimed in surprise, "how come I didn't hear about this?"

"It's really new," I joined in the conversation again. "He was just arrested last night."

"What for?"

"Trafficking women," I answered right away.

"More like running a brothel." Alon found it necessary to soften the felony a little. He gave me a menacing look to prevent me from adding any further description of that brothel and the imprisonment of the women inside.

"I imagine I'll hear about it from my staff on Sunday. What's so urgent?"

"The guy who's handling the case... Levinger, what's his name?"

"Attorney Idan Margolin," I answered.

"A bright guy, very thorough," she put in.

"Too thorough," he added immediately. "Which is exactly why I'm calling you at such an hour. I don't disregard, God forbid, the importance of the judicial process and of the agreement you'll sign with the witness -"

"May I please have his name?" she interrupted him. Except for Alon's ex-wife, I did not know many women who dared to interrupt him.

"Itzik Levayev."

"I haven't heard of him," she said right away.

"He has a criminal record, but he's not exactly a big fish," explained Alon.

"This is because he knows how to sign the right agreements with the D.A.," I added immediately.

"He's already been a state's witness in two or three previous cases," added Alon, having no other choice, and looked at me in a manner that made it clear I should keep quiet. "None of them was on this scale."

"Alright," she said. "So what's the problem with Attorney Margolin?"

"There's no problem," Alon tried fawning. "He made a great impression on me as well. It's just that he thinks that it'll take him two weeks to close a deal with Levayev, while I think your office can do it a lot faster."

"Listen, it doesn't depend just on us... He has a lawyer, for sure, who'll make demands – "

"Edna." It was Alon's turn to interrupt her. "We're in this business together, and we both know that such deals can be closed in a lot less than two weeks, if you really want to. This is not a state's witness who can close a twenty-year-old murder case; it's an open murder case, a case under ongoing investigation. The murderer's at large, and to the best of my knowledge, at this point he doesn't even know that Levayev's under arrest and is considering testifying against him. There's a certain urgency here you don't find in any old case."

"You're right," she said in a conciliatory tone. "Let me see what I can do."

"I'm counting on you, Edna," he replied in a tone I never heard from him before. "I must question this witness next week."

"Fine," she concluded in an utterly softened tone, almost seductively.

What the hell goes on at the D.A.'s fundraisers? I wondered.

"Edna." Once again, he switched to a tone that was completely new to me. This time he rolled her name in his mouth at a provocatively slow pace. "I'm going to be daring..." he fell dramatically silent. Edna started giggling. I felt embarrassed down to my toes; I had never witnessed such an odd flirtation. "I need it by Sunday... Monday at the latest," concluded Alon, his tone sweeter than honey.

She stopped giggling at once. "What are you on?" she asked, and he responded with boisterous laughter.

"Believe me, considering what I see here every day, it wouldn't hurt me to take a little something to escape from reality."

"I believe you." She was fawning again now.

"Then, really - make it happen. We're under insane pressure with this case. Imagine what'll happen if a snooping reporter discovers we had a State's witness, but failed to catch the murderer just because we held back on the agreement."

"Alright, alright," she sighed. "I can't promise you Sunday, but I'll do everything I can to push it through by Monday or Tuesday."

CHAPTER 10

By Sunday, almost all our detainees had been released. We had no evidence to tie them to the murder, and in any case, we did not try to convince the court to extend their detention. It didn't bother Alon. He was walking around as if the case was already closed and he just needed the phone call from the D.A.'s office. The more the hours passed and the phone call did not arrive, the more edgy he became. I tried to remind him that Edna had made it clear it would be impossible to close the deal on Sunday, but I knew that Alon was incapable of hearing a reasonable statement when he was edgy.

When the longed-for phone call did not arrive on Monday either, Alon reached a new level of agitation. He forced me to call Idan Margolin three times, in his presence, knowing that I would not call unless he was standing right next to me. He forced me to dictate my phone number to Idan, and extricate from him an oath that, the moment there was an agreement, he would call to let me know, even if the agreement was signed at an unsociable hour. Margolin said that the agreement was on the verge of being signed, and that we need only have a little patience. The problem was that Alon didn't have even one ounce of patience.

Eventually he called Edna Kahana himself. She screened his call.

Tuesday, June 21, 2011

I arrived at my office at a reasonable time in the morning. No phone call from Idan, no message from the D.A.'s office. However, another message was waiting on my desk. I was asked to call Dr. Amrani from the ICU at the Ichilov Hospital.

After a short trail of being transferred from one extension to another, I heard a man's voice: "Dr. Amrani."

"Shalom, Doctor. This is Inspector Hadas Levinger from the Central District. You left me a message to get back to you."

"You're investigating the murder last week at the Café Zelda?"

"Right."

"I was asked to let you know when Yoav Gottlieb regained consciousness."

Yoav was a barman at the Zelda snack bar. He had been standing near Shirley and was badly hit, but fortunately for him, not fatally.

"How is he?"

"Not great, but he's out of danger."

"Great."

"Yes, he was very lucky."

"Did he sustain any brain damage?"

"Are you asking if his memory was damaged? Well, it's still hard to know, but the tests we've conducted so far don't indicate any memory problems. With regard to the emotional difficulty, it's clear he's suffered severe trauma."

"I understand your sensitivity, but we must collect any piece of information he may have about that incident. In your opinion, is he up to answering a few questions?"

The doctor was silent for several seconds, and then said, "I assume he'll be able to handle a few brief questions."

He gave me the details of Yoav's room, and I got organized for the trip to the hospital.

When I was on my way out, Alon caught me. He was glowing with happiness, but frowned suddenly when he noticed the bag on my shoulder.

"Where do you think you're going?"

"To Ichilov. Yoav Gottlieb woke up."

"Who?"

"The injured barman from Café Zelda."

"Ah," he said indifferently. "Go later or send someone else."

"What is it now, Alon?"

"You really have to ask?! I just got a call from Edna Kahana! Itzik Levayev is all yours."

"Really?!" I, too, did not really stop to think twice. I did not think for a moment that Alon would pull one over on me about this. In my heart, I cursed Idan Margolin, who had not bothered to inform me about the developments.

"What? You think I'm joking here?" Another rhetorical question was thrown into the air. "Why didn't your friend at the D.A.'s office update you like he promised?"

"I've no idea," I said angrily and pulled my cell phone out of my bag. On the display, I saw a notification about a missed call from Attorney Margolin. "Oh. He did call me - ten minutes ago."

"Then why the hell didn't you return his call?"

"Enough, Alon!" I burst out. "You surely don't expect

me to go to the bathroom with my cell phone, right? You only just received the news yourself."

Alon was not used to me getting angry. He was not used to anyone answering him back at all, but, apparently, he realized that he was not the only one on edge.

"Fine, fine," he said in a conciliatory tone. "The main thing is that you don't burn a few good hours in Ichilov, now that you can finally talk to our dear Mr. Levayev."

"Shall I send someone else to the hospital?"

"I'll check if anyone's free. If not, you can go over there later, or even tomorrow. The most important thing is to interrogate our witness. Now."

"Certainly," I said and almost saluted him.

A little while later, I was again sitting in the interrogation room across from Itzik Levayev. The four days he had spent in the detention center had definitely left their mark on him. He was unshaven, his hair was disheveled, he was pale, and black circles decorated his eyes. His arrogant, self-satisfied attitude was gone as well. I placed a bottle of mineral water on the table in front of him wordlessly. A sealed one.

He smiled silently and pulled the bottle toward him.

"Mr. Levayev," I broke the silence. "Do you know why we're sitting here?"

"Yes."

"Very well. I'm going to say it for the protocol. This morning you signed a State's witness agreement in which you undertook to provide us with the identity of the murderer in the double murder that took place on Monday June 13, 2011 at Café Zelda in Tel-Aviv. Are these facts clear and agreed upon?"

"Yes," he almost whispered.

"A little louder, please. You know our conversation's being recorded."

He cleared his throat. "Sorry. Yes, everything's clear and acknowledged."

I smiled. "So, if everything's clear to all parties, let's get straight to the point. Who's the man we're looking for?"

"His name is Nagusto."

"Nagusto what?"

"Nagusto," he repeated.

"What sort of a name is that? A nickname?"

"No, that's his name."

"Is he Israeli?"

"No. He's a refugee from Eritrea."

"Okay. What's his last name?"

"I've no idea."

"You must be joking. Soon you'll be telling me you don't know where he lives, either."

"Nobody knows where he lives," he said.

I chuckled aloud.

"I'm giving you the name of a hired hitman, not a bank clerk," he said angrily. "I may not know his passport number - if he has a passport at all, but I know for certain that it's him. And I also know more or less where he hangs out. So I *am* sure." He paused for a moment and then corrected himself. "That is, I hope you'll manage to track him down."

His unconcealed criticism was not at all pleasing to my ears.

"Alright," I said. "Let's assume we'll be able to track him down. Now tell me how you know him exactly and why you think he's the killer."

"Nagusto's the type everybody's heard about - that is, everybody in the vicinity of the old Central Station - but nobody really knows who he is. If you ask me, I'm not even sure that's his real name, and I don't know if there's anyone who knows his last name. I met him in the club.

He used to come at least once a week and take at least one girl. He had needs, as people say." Itzik winked at me and I shuddered. "There are quite a few whores from Eritrea and Sudan. The girls who come from there need every penny they can earn and are a lot cheaper than my girls, but he loved white meat." I couldn't help rolling my eyes. The thought that the judicial system would not persecute this pimp according to the letter of the law drove me crazy.

"I don't know exactly how old he is, but he's quite young. Very tall, well built."

The description corresponded to the testimonies we had collected from eye witnesses to the murder. They had described a tall, robust guy wearing a helmet, which explained why he had not been described as dark skinned.

"He was one of the first refugees to arrive in South Tel-Aviv. I've known him at least two years. He liked eating at the restaurant above the club."

"The restaurant that burned down?"

"Yes," he said and gnashed his teeth. That was the fire that had led to his arrest. He did not like remembering it. Several minutes passed before Itzik resumed talking smoothly.

"I talked with him a little. His parents were killed during the Eritrean War of Independence. Several years later, his uncles decided to escape to Israel and he joined them. In Israel, he tried those jobs the Eritreans take - you know, cleaning, kitchens, and such. But it didn't suit him. He was broken. He saw his parents die when he was just a kid and it probably messed up his head. I don't know how he started killing people for money, but it simply happened."

"So he's an active hit man for hire?"

"Yes."

"How do you know?"

"Nobody really knows, but let's just say he's not the type you'd want to meet down a dark alley. He's massive, and he hardly speaks, but when he does speak, he has a very deep voice. It reverberates."

"Does he speak Hebrew?"

"Fluently, with a slight accent. The guy has brains, he just didn't have much luck in his life. He picked up the language easily."

"Does he have any distinguishing features?"

Itzik thought for a moment and then jumped up. "Yes! Sure! Why didn't I think of it before? He has a tattoo of flames on his face."

"Over his entire face?"

"No, only on one side. The right side, I think."

"Like the one Mike Tyson has?"

"No, it's the same style, but not the same."

"I still don't understand why you're sure he's a hit man for hire in general, and the murderer from Café Zelda in particular?"

"He's smart, that's why he hasn't been caught. The rumors about him are well-founded. I don't know exactly how old he is, maybe twenty-four, something like that, but for a guy that age, he lives very well. Definitely very well for an Eritrean immigrant. He has a brand-new motorbike -"

"What model?" I cut him off in the hope of corroborating the information with the testimonies of the eye witnesses.

"No... I really don't understand such things. I've seen him riding it once or twice. I know about the motorbike because he used to arrive at the club with the helmet. He wears branded designer gear, not the shit sold around the

Central Station. Good shoes, designer watch. He always left tips for the girls. He has plenty of money, but nobody knows where he works. People only know it's better not to mess with him. You want a story? Here's a story: his uncle cuts off all contact with him because he's ashamed of him. But his aunt, who actually raised him after his parents died, she can't cut him off. Long story short - she's shopping in her regular minimarket, and when she gets to the checkout, she discovers her purse is gone! She begs the cashier, who knows her, to let her take the groceries and bring the money later, but he won't agree and makes her leave the store full of shame. Next day, two things happen: the cashier's got a cast on his left hand, and Nagusto's aunt gets a fifteen percent discount for her shopping in the minimarket - for life. This is Nagusto. These are the stories they tell about him. Everyone knows he does all kinds of hand-breaking and leg-breaking jobs for the crime families."

"Breaking hands and legs isn't exactly being a hired hitman," I hurried to correct him.

"Right. But how many crime families are satisfied with breaking hands and legs?" he retorted.

"Well, then, tell me how you know he's the killer from Café Zelda."

"A day before the murder, he was in my club. I can't say it for sure, but I gotta feeling that, before a job, he had to come to us. Maybe to calm down or something like that."

"And except for this 'feeling,' do you have anything more solid to establish this theory?"

"He looked very tense. And he got a call, and he answered it quietly - not like him."

"Fine, continue."

"In short - a day before the murder... when was that?"

"The murder was last Monday."

"So, last Sunday he's at my club. He asks for Anya, his favorite. But she's with another customer. He says he'll wait, and in the meantime, he gets a call."

"Did you hear the call?"

"I only heard what he said. It was very brief, and the truth is that without the murder the next day, I wouldn't have noticed anything special about that call."

Itzik took a long pause, sipped some water, looked at my alert eyes and continued. "He repeated what the other party was saying and asked me for a pen and paper to write it down." Itzik stopped.

"Well, what did they tell him that he had to write down?" I had to take part in his game.

"He said 'Café Zelda at half twelve.' They asked him if he knew the address, and he said he knew where it was and hung up."

I was silent. The entire occurrence Itzik described was totally circumstantial. Still, there were too many clues that Nagusto, or whatever the guy's name was, was indeed the man we were looking for.

I knew that Alon, who was watching and listening to the entire interrogation, was mentally opening a bottle of champagne. I hoped he was not celebrating too soon.

"How come you remember exactly what Nagusto said in such a short conversation?" I asked Itzik, trying to sound skeptical.

"I remember it so well for two reasons. One, when he says the name of the place, it sounds strange to me. Because I know that snack bar, I've been there once or twice, and it's not exactly the sort of place where the guys from Eritrea hang out. More of a place for smart snobs from North Tel-Aviv. This is one. Two, the following day, when I hear about the murder, I connect

Nagusto's conversation to the hit right away. No way was it just a coincidence."

I agreed.

I let Itzik wait in the hallway and sent for Anya. If the poor woman was Nagusto's favorite, she should be able to describe him well. After a short interview, I called in our facial composite artist. Anya and Itzik described Nagusto, and the artist did a good job. The facial composite was intended for a special squad we had created. The squad was sent to five locations in the area of the old Central Station - places Nagusto frequented, according to Itzik's information. The squad members were instructed not to question the local people and not to show the facial composite to anybody. We knew it would not be simple. We had information about five locations, but not enough manpower to visit all of them simultaneously. For this reason, we instructed the team to move from one location to another and risk losing the target. But there was no other choice. Nagusto had to be unaware that the police were looking for him. The element of surprise was crucial.

CHAPTER 11

Thursday, June 23, 2011

Two days passed and we still hadn't located Nagusto. Alon, as usual, had not an ounce of patience. The undercover squad reported that the closure of Itzik's club had reverberated throughout the neighborhood. I explained to Alon that it made sense for tough guys like Nagusto to disappear. I moved between the undercover teams, and joined one long and tiring watch in the restaurant above Itzik Levayev's closed brothel. There were several false alarms, which drove up our pulse rates, but left us disappointed.

Nagusto had simply vanished.

The more the hours passed, the more I sensed that the guy had realized he was a marked man, and that the closure of Itzik's club and his arrest had been a warning sign for him as well. The increased presence of uniformed cops after the incident did not help either, even though, theoretically, Nagusto had nothing to fear. He had no police record and was not connected to the club management.

The pressure was not helping me or the investigation. I decided to get away from South Tel-Aviv for a few hours, and go to the Ichilov Hospital to finally question Yoav Gottlieb, the injured waiter who had regained consciousness. Since the entire manpower of the police station had been allocated to the search for Nagusto and to the ongoing tasks, nobody had found the time to do it yet.

The switch to Central Tel-Aviv after two days of walking around the rundown area of the old Central Station was like landing on Mars: big, new buildings, brand name stores, clean people dressed in the latest fashions – light years from the gloomy squalor that was the reality just a few kilometers from there.

Once inside the hospital, I channeled my route with efficient speed, thanks to the precise instructions provided by Dr. Amrani. Otherwise, I would have been lost in the maze of light green corridors, where each corridor was identical to the next. Thus, I arrived at the trauma ward. The ward staff were preoccupied with their work, the hospitalized patients and their families were absorbed in their affairs, and nobody asked me why I was standing at the door of Room 523, a private room assigned to the wounded recuperating from severe injuries. The door was half open. I knocked gently and did not hear a response. I tiptoed into the room. If Yoav was asleep, it would be better for me not to wake him up. However, the bed was empty. I looked around and realized that the room was being prepared to receive a new patient. The bed sheets were new and spread tight, the dresser next to the bed was clean, and there was nothing in the room to indicate that a patient had been hospitalized there. Had he been transferred to another ward, or had something else happened?

I turned around to leave and bumped into a young, energetic nurse who had just entered the room.

"Can I ask who you are and what you're doing here?" she asked, surprised. I flashed my badge at her. She was not startled. After all, she was a nurse in the trauma ward. I assumed she had already met a cop or two in here.

"My name's Hadas Levinger. Dr. Amrani called me two days ago and said I could visit Yoav Gottlieb. He gave me this room number."

"He's been transferred," she said as she placed a hospital pajama set and matching bathrobe on the bed.

"Where can I find him now?"

"I'll have to check with Dr. Amrani first." She smiled a false smile.

"No problem," I smiled too. "Where is he?"

"I think he already left," she said and looked hesitant for a moment. Then her face softened. "Come with me to the nurses' station," she said and invited me with a gesture. "I'll call him."

After a short conversation with Dr. Amrani, I was led to Yoav Gottlieb's new room. On the way there, the nurse told me that Yoav had been transferred to a regular room with two other patients due to the considerable improvement in his condition.

We entered the room. The sound of light snoring came from one bed. A guy was lying there, asleep. Next to his bed was a small sofa where a young woman was curled up, also asleep. The second bed was empty, and in the third, a guy was reading a book. The nurse pointed at the reading guy, told me it was the person I was looking for, and left.

I approached him.

"Yoav?" I asked in a whisper, afraid of waking the sleeping couple.

He raised his eyes from the book and looked at me,

surprised.

"Shalom. My name's Hadas Levinger. I'm a policewoman with the Israel Police," I said and showed my badge.

This time, it made an impression. Yoav gaped, then smiled in embarrassment. He understood why I was there.

"Yes, Dr. Amrani told me someone would come to interrogate me."

"To question you," I corrected him. I did not want him to feel intimidated.

"No problem," he smiled. He was a very handsome guy. I could see it even through the scratches and bruises covering his face. I could easily visualize him standing behind the counter of the fashionable café just a week and a half earlier, serving lawyers, businessmen and Tel-Aviv hipsters.

"The nurse said we could talk in Dr. Amrani's office," I said. In answer to his questioning look, I rushed to add, "We must speak in private."

"No problem. I just need a bit of help. I can't get out of bed by myself and at present I'm using a wheelchair."

"You want me to help you?" I asked, a little terrified. I had no previous experience helping injured patients get out of bed or anything like that.

"No, no, of course not," he hurried to calm me down and buzzed the nurse.

A few minutes later, we were sitting alone in Dr. Amrani's office.

"First of all, how do you feel?" I asked politely. Two months earlier, a police psychologist had come to our station to conduct a workshop on human relationships. I recalled her advice to be warmer toward people being interrogated who have not been charged with anything.

"I've had better days," he smiled a twisted smile. "But,

thank God, I got out of it alive."

"Yes. I understand you were in bad shape, but you're recuperating very nicely."

"Right."

"I'm glad to hear that. According to what the doctor told me, you've avoided brain damage, and your memory's working perfectly."

"I think so. That is, I hope so."

I took my tape recorder out of my bag and notified Yoav that, from that moment on, our conversation was being recorded.

He nodded and I pressed the record button.

"With your permission, let's return to the day of the incident," I said gently. "Where exactly were you standing when the shooting started?"

"Right behind the counter, where I usually stand."

"What do you do at Café Zelda?"

"I take out the hot and cold drinks, and I'm also in charge of the cash register."

"What were you doing before the shooting?"

"I'd just brought out a takeaway order from the kitchen."

"Was it Shirley Navon's order? The girl who was murdered?"

"Yes."

"Do you happen to remember Koby Ozri, the man who also died? He was sitting at the table near the counter."

"Truthfully, no. I mainly talk to the waiters and people who come over to take a coffee or a delivery directly from the counter. The ones who sit at a table make contact with the waiters, so I had no reason to speak with him."

"Do you know the steady customers? Even those who usually sit at a table?"

"Sure."

"But you didn't know Koby."

"No."

"Then, can I conclude that he wasn't a regular customer of yours?"

"To the best of my memory, it was the first time I'd seen him at our place. That is, I don't remember seeing him before. I've seen his picture in the paper and on TV, but I don't recall seeing him at our place, so I assume it was the first time he'd been."

"Alright. Do people make reservations at your place?"

"You mean reserve a table?"

"Yes." I was hoping that the initiator of the assassination had reserved the table for Koby.

"No." He shook his head. "That is, sometimes people call and ask if it's necessary to reserve a space, but we don't take reservations. If there's no space, people can wait until a table becomes available."

This did not help. According to all the eyewitnesses, Koby was sitting by himself. The waitress who approached him a few minutes before the shooting said that he had asked her to wait with his order because he was waiting for somebody. For whom?

My working assumption was that the person who made the appointment to meet Koby at Zelda's was the same one who hired Nagusto to carry out the assassination. It was highly unlikely that the person who invited Koby to the café would have shown up, but I still asked, "Do you know if anybody joined Koby at the table?"

"I don't remember," he admitted. "I take care of the counter mainly and don't deal with the tables."

Damn it, this witness was not providing me with any new information. I was already regretting leaving the old Central Station area.

"Let's proceed to the shooting itself," I said in order to

complete the interrogation report. I was not going to obtain any genuine information about Koby's fateful meeting.

Yoav steadied himself by holding onto the back of his wheelchair and taking a deep breath.

"Is that okay?" I asked in the most soothing tone of voice I could muster.

"Yes," he said in the least reliable tone of voice he could muster. "I gather I don't have much of a choice."

"You'll have to talk about it eventually." I smiled reassuringly; "I think it's better to be done with it."

"Alright, let's try."

"Describe to me, please, the moments before the shooting itself."

"As I told you, just before the shooting started, I brought out the order for Shirley, God rest her soul. As far as I remember, we were going over the order to make sure it was correct and then the shooting began."

"Do you remember how many shots were fired?"

"No, but there were several, not one or two."

In the search we conducted on site, we had found eight slugs.

"Did you happen to see the shooter?"

"Yes. In my opinion, this was my mistake. When I heard the first shot, I didn't think it was aimed at us at all. So I raised my head, looked out, and saw him. In my opinion, if I'd ducked down, I wouldn't have been injured like that."

"How far from you was he?"

"Just across the sidewalk. I think… something like ten meters."

"If I showed you his picture, or if we held a line-up, do you think you'd be able to identify him?"

"Not a chance. He was wearing a motorcycle helmet."

"Then what did you see?"

"Not much. The moment I realized he was shooting, it was too late. He approached me and continued shooting."

"What do you mean - 'approached me'?"

"He walked straight toward me, shooting."

"Are you telling me he was aiming at you?"

"No way! What connection do I have with him?!" Yoav was scared just by the thought that he had a direct connection to the incident.

"You probably know already that Koby Ozri was a former felon and an active police informer."

"So I heard."

"But you're telling me that the shooter was shooting in your direction and not at Koby."

Yoav breathed deeply. "I don't understand anything about the world of crime and about police matters, but if you ask me, that man was shooting at Shirley. That's why I was wounded so badly."

I made a great effort to hide my surprise. These words could turn around the entire investigation. Up to that moment, I had assumed that Shirley was an innocent victim of unfortunate circumstances.

"Do you mean to tell me that the shooter killed Shirley Navon on purpose?"

"I'm almost certain he did," he said, and bit his lip. "Almost certain... uh... you... uh... you've got to understand that it was a matter of seconds, and I'm not exactly used to such situations. But I remember it quite well. It's actually the last thing I remember of the entire incident, before one of his bullets hit me and I lost consciousness."

"Which means there's no point me asking you if you saw him shoot Koby..."

"No. It must have happened after he shot Shirley and me. That is, he shot Shirley, I'm almost certain about that. I was simply hit by accident. I remember clearly that he was holding his gun up straight and pointed it - actually aimed it - at Shirley."

"Did you know Shirley? Was she a steady customer?"

"She came in once in a while."

"To eat in? Take out?"

"Both. She worked at one of the offices nearby, as far as I know."

"She worked at Panda."

"That's right!" He smiled. "She brought us branded gifts on Passover. Charming girl."

"Yes. This is what I understand from her parents, as well." I thought about Shirley's father, how agitated he had been by his daughter's tragic and inadvertent death. Was her death really a terrible mistake? The testimony I had just heard was intriguing and unusual, but entirely illogical. I found it hard to believe that Shirley Navon, a young student, had been a target of the underworld. Still, there was no way I could disregard this testimony. I would have to consider other investigative directions. Everything would be a lot simpler if we could finally track down the killer and interrogate him.

After taking my leave from Yoav, I entered the comfortable, air-conditioned Weitzman Mall. I decided that my digestive system deserved something less challenging than the food offered by the questionable food stalls in the Central Station area, so I sat down in an Aroma Café franchise.

While I was eating and leafing through the daily issue of *Israel Today*, a female voice addressed me. "Excuse me?"

I raised my eyes; it was a young woman with the round belly of pregnancy. "May I take this chair?" She pointed at the empty chair next to me.

"Sure," I said with a full mouth. She smiled with gratitude. There was something pleasant and soft about her. She caressed her belly and held her back with her other hand for a moment, the way many pregnant women did, I'd noticed. It was probably due to the backache that came along with pregnancy. "Wait up!" I almost shouted when I realized that she intended to pick up the chair and take it away. "Let me help you."

"There's no need," she smiled, embarrassed.

"Nonsense. Where do you want it?" I asked. She pointed at a nearby table.

"Thank you," she said and sat down. "In fact, I've just come from the clinic. They told me to rest up. So you've been really helpful. Thank you."

"No problem," I smiled. "My pleasure. Do you need me to bring you your order from the counter?"

"No," she laughed. "The extra chair's for my husband. Here he is, with our order." She pointed over my shoulder.

I turned around.

It was Yinon.

CHAPTER 12

It took both of us a while to come to our senses. We simply stood in front of each other with a frozen look, not knowing what to say or do.

"Hi," I said to break the odd silence.

"What are you doing here?" he asked.

"Eating lunch."

He shook his head. "No. I meant what are you doing here, next to our table?"

By this time, Orit had already internalized that we were not strangers. "You know each other?" she asked, but we were busy being startled, so her question hung in the air.

"I'm sitting over there," I pointed to my table. "I helped Orit bring you a chair."

"Thank you," he smiled and recalled that he had to perform a round of introductions. He put down the tray of sandwiches and coffee on the table and introduced me to Orit. "Orit, may I introduce Hadas, my ex-wife."

"What?!" Her eyes opened wide in incredulity. "What a coincidence."

For a moment, it looked like Orit was going to introduce herself, but Yinon was ahead of her. "Orit's my partner," he said, his eyes shifting sideways. I knew him. He wanted to escape, but had nowhere to go. "And as you see, we're pregnant."

"I heard about it," I said and released him from his agony.

"How?"

"I met Revital a few days ago and she told me."

"She didn't tell me she'd bumped into you."

"Are you in such a close relationship?" I wondered.

"I'm quite close to Ronen. Well, maybe they didn't imagine we'd run into each other. So, well, now you can see for yourself, not just hear about it."

"My pleasure," I smiled at Orit and extended my hand to her. She pressed it feebly.

"I was actually wondering why a woman would be walking around with a gun, but Yinon told me you're a policewoman."

"That's right."

"Perhaps you'll join us?" she suggested. "I noticed you only just started eating."

"With pleasure," I said. I was curious. I wanted to get to know Orit and also to speak with Yinon.

We joined our tables together and I returned to my pasta dish.

"Now that I know who you are, I can see you really look like the pictures Yinon showed me," Orit said and examined me thoroughly.

"I don't look my best today," I said. "I've been on surveillance for two days."

Orit gaped in curiosity. She placed her elbows on the table and held her chin in the palms of her hands. She was all ears and excited. "Really? You don't say! Who are you following?"

"I can't talk about it."

She ignored what I said. "Is it someone here? At the hospital?"

"No."

"Is everything alright with you?" Yinon asked with concern that warmed my heart.

"Yes. Why are you asking?"

"Well, you're in the café attached to the hospital…"

"Everything's alright," I smiled and rushed to change the direction of the conversation. "And what about you two? Are you alright?"

"The doctors say everything's normal," said Orit.

"Did something happen to give you cause for concern?"

"Orit tends to faint during pregnancy," Yinon put in.

"And this is considered normal?"

"Everything's alright!" Orit burst in before Yinon could get a word in. "Yinon worries too much."

I wanted Yinon to be concerned about me again, but his concerned gaze was focused on Orit and her round belly. "How many months?"

"I'm in the twenty-ninth week." I stared at her with a hollow gaze.

"The seventh month," translated Yinon.

Orit related the challenges of her pregnancy and I was as bored as I had ever been during any conversation about this topic with any girlfriend or with my sisters. She complained to me that Yinon was too worried about her and too protective, as if there was some sort of a womanly camaraderie between the two of us – Yinon's women. I finished eating quickly and got up. "I must get back to work. Good luck with everything," I said and left, almost running.

The encounter with Yinon was not as difficult as it was embarrassing and onerous. Though I had already known that he was in a new relationship and expecting a child, the encounter with him unsettled me completely.

I returned to South Tel-Aviv, but could not concentrate

on anything. Orit told me she had seen my picture,
which meant that Yinon had kept my pictures, at least
one of them. I had thrown away all my pictures of him. I
did not want to remember him, and, with time, his image
had started to fade in my memory. It was so odd seeing
him again. Face to face. He had not changed much -
"Are you alright?" Someone cut off my train of thought.
Shachar, my colleague.
"So-so... I'm tired, I guess."
"Then go home. I'll fill in for you," suggested Shachar.
Unusually for me, I accepted his offer and drove home.
I heard Tsumi's joyful barking as soon as I reached the
entrance to my apartment building. Why was he barking
like that? I turned on the light in the stairwell and
noticed someone lying on my doorstep. I drew my hand
to my gun automatically. As I drew closer, the person
got up.
It was Yinon.
"What are you doing here?" I asked, opening the door.
"I had to talk to you," he said and followed me into the
apartment without asking my permission.
Tsumi leaped on us in a series of excited jumps and
licking. He was barking with enthusiasm and skipped
happily from me to Yinon, like a little child whose
parents have finally gotten back together. Yinon bent
down and hugged the dog warmly.
"Does he need to go out?" he asked.
"He was walked by the neighbors' daughter this
afternoon. I'll take him later."
Yinon wanted to get up from the floor, but as far as
Tsumi was concerned, there was no chance of that, and
after so many months of separation, he would not be
satisfied with a brief petting. The pleasure-seeking dog
rolled over and Yinon started to pet his stomach. After a

few minutes, he left the dog and followed me into the kitchen.

"Do you bathe him sometimes?" he asked, washing his hands, which were black from the lengthy massage he had given Tsumi.

"Once in a while," I answered impatiently. "Do you want anything to eat? I'm making myself a toastie with Swiss cheese."

"No, thanks. I'll get myself something to drink, though," he said and opened the refrigerator as casually as if it were his own. He looked at the bare shelves in my refrigerator for a long moment. Finally, he took out a near-empty container of orange juice and poured it into a clean glass he found in the cabinet.

"My refrigerator's usually less empty," I tried to justify myself. "I'm simply in the midst of a high-pressure investigation."

"Are you still working with that Alon?"

"Yes."

"I think it's abnormal to live like this."

"Sorry. I haven't read the Guide for Normal Life," I said, and he laughed.

"I mean, getting home late like this, eating irregularly. It doesn't seem healthy to me."

"Since we were married for several years, I remember you too, like many other common high-tech slaves, coming home late."

"But at least I eat healthy food regularly."

"I assume Orit takes care of it."

"She does. She's into home cooking."

"So you've settled down."

Yinon was silent. He looked at me, his eyes full of anger - or guilt. I could not decipher it. After all, we had not been together for several years, and had not seen each other at all for over a year-and-a-half.

"I had to speak with you," he said. "I've wanted to contact you for a long time, but I simply didn't have an opportunity."

"Did you lose my phone number?"

"I couldn't manage to call you," he said, embarrassed. "It's hard for me," he added, his voice trembling.

"Yinon, you don't have to ask my permission to date another woman," I said in the most encouraging tone I could manage. The Swiss cheese in the toastie machine started to bubble. I turned it off and put the sandwich on a plate. "Let's go in the living room," I suggested and went to sit on the sofa.

Yinon sat opposite me and finished the rest of the juice in his glass in one gulp. "It's important for me that you understand what happened. Last time we spoke, we parted from each other in tears, and less than two years later you meet me with a pregnant woman."

"Yinon, we talked about this about a billion times. This was exactly the reason for our separation: you wanted kids, I didn't. It's your right to find yourself another woman and have kids with her," I said. In fact, I was trying to convince myself.

"So you're completely fine with it?"

"I won't lie to you. I took it hard when Revital told me about it. But, after all, I knew this day would come."

"I'm really sorry you had to find out like that," he said and got up to put the empty glass in the sink. For a moment I was afraid, or hoped, that he would come back and sit next to me, but he returned to his seat. "I really wanted to contact you, but it was hard for me. Orit's had a lot of problems with the pregnancy, so I truly couldn't find the right time."

"Are you married?"

"Not yet."

"Not yet?"

"We thought about getting married early on in the pregnancy, when she wasn't showing yet. But Orit was sick all the time and it was hard for her to organize it. I suggested we get married in the office of the Rabbinate, but she wanted a wedding in a banquet hall, the white dress, all her friends and all that."

"How old is she?"

"Twenty-eight."

"Then she's at an age when the party's important to her."

"You were also twenty-eight when we got married, but the party didn't really interest you," he reminded me.

The real reason I registered at the Rabbinate, wore a white dress and smiled forced smiles for an entire evening had been the knowledge that my parents would not have given me the money for an apartment without the Rabbinate's seal. Since, fundamentally, I had nothing against the institution of marriage, and since I knew that Yinon really, really wanted a wedding, I went along with it. When nobody could see or hear me, I could even admit to myself that I enjoyed it.

"But, the fact is, we did have a wedding - the full works," I smiled.

He smiled back. "We had a beautiful wedding."

"It really was."

"In any case, the party's really important for Orit," he continued.

"And for you?"

"I admit, less so…"

"So why are you two planning to do it, then?"

"I don't think she should give up something that's so important to her. In any case, it won't be a big event."

He stopped for a moment and tried to organize his

thoughts. "Wait up, I'm getting things confused here. I want to begin at the beginning."

"You can begin wherever you want."

"I want to tell you exactly how it started, so you understand that it was all very fortuitous."

"You don't have to explain anything to me."

"But I want to," he said. "I think the last time I was here, the pain in my hip joint had just started giving me some trouble. Do you remember it?"

"I remember something." I remembered perfectly well. It was another innocent meeting that had ended between the sheets. Yinon made a wrong move and cried out in pain. I cried in panic. A few days after that, we decided to stop seeing each other.

"I went to an orthopedist and he recommended Pilates. I signed up at the gym near my home and I met Orit there."

"Yes, I heard from Revital that Orit's a Pilates instructor."

"Right."

"This was truly how we met. I didn't register on a dating site, and she wasn't introduced to me by someone trying to fix me up. People tried to fix me up with women incessantly. They wouldn't stop bugging me to join dating sites, but it was hard for me." He lowered his eyes. "It was difficult for me to take steps that meant the termination of our relationship. I gather... although we decided to cut off any contact between us, I still hoped..." He raised his eyes and I noticed they were glistening.

"In any case, the moment I met Orit, things just started happening on their own. More accurately, they happened because Orit had made them happen. I don't know. Maybe if I was looking for a relationship today, it might have been another girl. I admit I wasn't ripe and ready, but she accepted me the way I was."

"Did she know about me?"

"She knows I was married before and the reason we separated, but not a lot more. She doesn't like asking about you, and I don't like telling her."

"Does she know you're here now?"

"What?" he asked, horrified. "I slipped out after she fell asleep. She sleeps a lot now that she's pregnant."

"Well, she's sleeping for two," I laughed and Yinon joined me.

"I admit it's very flattering when a woman loves you like that," he continued. "And it's clear to me that Orit loves me a lot, otherwise she wouldn't have behaved the way she did. She didn't play games with me at all. Right away, she made it clear to me and to everybody around that she wanted me and wouldn't give up. I admit - it was appealing."

"You don't have to apologize."

"I'm not apologizing. I'm only telling you what happened. Two months after we met, she moved in with me. In fact, the circumstances sort of led up to it. Her lease was up and she had to leave her apartment. My apartment's near the gym, so it was quite logical for her to move in with me."

I smiled to myself. The girl simply marked her target and didn't give up.

"Six months after Orit had moved in with me, we found out about the baby coming. It was unplanned..." he hurried to explain.

I sighed inwardly. Yinon was so naïve. I had no doubt that the pregnancy *was* planned - but by only one party in that relationship.

"By the time we found out, Orit was already in the third

month. Her periods are irregular, so she didn't even know she was pregnant."

I made an effort not to burst out laughing. Even with my limited knowledge of female fertility, I knew that the third month was more or less the time when an abortion became impossible. The girl had it all planned.

"And how did you feel when you found out you were going to be a father?"

"Very excited," he answered, embarrassed. "I admit, it was hard to get used to the new relationship, but the thought that I was about to become a father simply stunned me. I'd waited for it so long." His eyes filled with tears.

I knew what he was thinking. He wanted this fetus to be in my belly. I also started to shed tears. I felt sorry for him, I felt sorry for myself and I cursed the impossible situation we had run into.

I got up and went over to him. He did not recoil from me. I sat down right next to him, almost on his knees, and hugged him affectionately. He returned the hug. We sat like that, hugging each other and weeping.

"I love you so much," he whispered suddenly in my ear and began to kiss me.

I broke away from him. "No... Yinon..." I muttered feebly, but he did not give up and clung to me again. I stood up.

"I don't want us to do something you'll regret later. You're about to start a family," I said and returned to sit on the opposite sofa.

He looked at me miserably.

"I want you to know..." he said and bit his lip, "you should know... I'm really happy to become a father."

"I've no doubt about it," I said gently.

"And Orit's a good girl."

"And that's why it's best you go home now."

"You're right," he said and got up.

I accompanied him to the door. "Let's keep in touch," I told him before he left.

"Are you sure about that? Will that be good - for us, I mean?"

"I don't know. But not being in touch isn't very good for us either, so just keep me updated on what's happening."

"Fine."

"Let me know when Orit gives birth."

"Fine."

"By the way, what are you having?"

"A boy."

"Best of luck."

"Amen," he said and went down the stairs, almost running.

CHAPTER 13

Friday, June 24, 2011

The meeting with Yinon was beneficial for me. The feeling of discomfort which had burdened me since finding out that he was in a new relationship and about to become a father disappeared as if it had never been. I knew that, in spite of everything, he was still mine and we had not stopped loving each other. It was frustrating and flattering at the same time. He wanted to be a father – so let him be a father. I could not know what the future had in store for us. I only knew that I could not let Yinon leave Orit while she was in the advanced stage of pregnancy.

I went down to the neighborhood café for a light breakfast. The tables were full, and the street was packed with people enjoying the sunny Friday morning. I definitely wanted to enjoy a relaxed and pleasant weekend as well, but I wanted even more to get a phone call telling me that Nagusto had been found. The top brass was eagerly awaiting results. There were those who already doubted the testimony of Itzik Levayev, but every ounce of my intuition told me that Itzik had not lied and had not made an error.

On the way home, I stopped at a deli and bought few sweet snacks for Shabbat. I told myself that, according to Murphy's Law, if I bought a lot of snacks for myself, I would not have the time to enjoy them, because Nagusto would be found and I would have to leave everything.

By noon, it became clear that Murphy had been right again.

I was lying in bed, sleepy, covered with the weekend papers and cheesecake crumbs, when the longed-for phone call woke me up. One of the teams had identified Nagusto almost positively. That team had localized in on a fairly popular Eritrean restaurant and was alerted when a man arrived on a motorcycle identical to that from the shooting at Zelda's.

The rider joined a group of young guys sitting in the restaurant and joined in their conversation. One of the cops took his picture with his cell phone and sent it to me. It was rather a good picture. I forwarded the picture to the officer on call at the police station so he could show it to Itzik Levayev. After fifteen minutes, we had confirmation.

We had found Nagusto.

I instructed the team to do nothing more than follow the man. It was not enough to catch him; I wanted to take him at home in order to find the gun with which he had executed the hit.

I shook off the papers and the crumbs and went out to the site. On the way, I got an update: Nagusto had left the restaurant, ridden his motorcycle for several hundred meters, and entered an old apartment building.

I asked the team to wait for me before entering the building. I wanted to supervise things myself. On my way there, I was informed that it was probably not Nagusto's home. Too many men were entering the building and leaving it. Nagusto, it turned out, was visiting a brothel to relieve his urges. After half an hour, he left again.

By that time, I had joined the surveillance team and finally got to see the man up close. He was an impressive man, tall and robust. His facial features were chiseled in straight lines, as if they were cast in a mold. I identified the tattoo Itzik had described. In my opinion, the tattoo marred his handsome face, but I figured Nagusto had wanted to add a tough or mysterious touch to his personality.

Nagusto climbed on his motorbike and drove to a mini-market on Har Zion Avenue. He entered the store and left several minutes later loaded with bags of snacks and alcoholic drinks. His next stop was a rundown public park, where a few young guys were waiting for him and welcomed him with joyful cries.

I passed the next few hours along with the team, staring at Nagusto and his friends. They were drinking, shouting, and fooling around until two a.m. The bunch finally dispersed and Nagusto got on his motorcycle, speeding away on almost empty roads. I had instructed Shachar to take advantage of Nagusto's visit to the brothel and attach a surveillance device to his motorcycle, so that following him would not turn into a chase that would lead us away from his home.

Now we could allow ourselves to follow him at a greater distance, while still actually knowing where he was at each moment. The surveillance device led us south, to one of the streets in a southern neighborhood of Yaffo, bordering with Holon. The Central Station area was like the Champs Élysées in comparison with this street. The row of single story houses was almost derelict. Most of them were composed of ramshackle patches of amateurish, piratical construction. Some of the dwellings were actually just converted shipping containers. The street was silent and dark, and only the small house where Nagusto's motorcycle was parked had any lights on. We peeked through one of the windows and saw our target lying on the sofa, playing on a PlayStation. The team comprised three more cops besides Shachar and me. We surrounded the house and prepared to break in.

I knocked on the door. I heard the volume of the television game lower and Nagusto approaching the door.

"Who is it?" he asked in fluent Hebrew.

"Police!" said Shachar in a decisive tone.

"Just a moment," he said. "I need to get dressed."

We knew that he was dressed and that the only thing he wanted to put on now was a gun. "We know you're dressed," said Shachar. "If you don't open up right now we'll break in."

"Alright, alright," he said and opened the door.

"Hands up!" ordered Shachar in Hebrew.

"Hands up!" I added in English when Nagusto did not obey immediately. I realized quickly that using English was unnecessary. Nagusto was perfectly fluent in Hebrew.

Nagusto's home was an old, crumbling structure. The paint was peeling from the walls and water leaks had left their mark on the ceiling. The floor was covered with stained, old tiles, most of them broken. In the center of the house was a living room. At one end of the living room, I saw an improvised kitchenette, and at the other end I saw two doors, one leading to a bathroom with a shower and the other to a tiny bedroom. The kitchenette was equipped with an old sink, a filthy stove, a noisy refrigerator and cabinets without doors. Against this wretchedness, a new, prestigious leather sofa, a gigantic television screen and state-of-the-art speaker system stood out. I did not recognize all the devices attached to the television screen, but I understood they were expensive game consoles. On the glass table between the sofa and the television were scattered boxes of games and porno movies.

Nagusto raised his hands and was led by a third cop toward one of the walls to be searched and handcuffed.

"I have a visitor visa," he kept muttering.

"We're not Immigration," I told him. "Do you have a passport? Documents?"

Nagusto led us to the bedroom, which was also dilapidated and dingy. Nagusto's passport was in the closet. The old closet was jam packed with brand-name jeans and shirts, some of which still had their tags on. I opened the drawer Nagusto pointed at and found a treasure trove of scores of watches, rings and necklaces. Underneath all of that was the passport.

"Nagusto Gorgodsa," I read aloud from the passport. Now I knew that "Nagusto" was not a nickname. I looked at the documents tucked into the passport. Nagusto did, indeed, have a legal visitor visa. He was twenty-three and had arrived in Israel six years earlier, after crossing the Sinai Peninsula on foot. He had the status of a war refugee. Very few Eritreans had managed to get such a status, which granted him a free and secure stay in Israel. From the document attached to the visitor visa, I learned that Nagusto had been orphaned at age eight, and that several years later he had joined his uncles on the long journey from Eritrea to Israel.

"I told you I was legal," he repeated. His Hebrew was perfect, with a barely an accent.

"And I told you we're not from Immigration," I said and

led him back to the living room.

An additional police vehicle arrived on the scene, and Nagusto was handcuffed inside it. One cop remained in the vehicle to watch him, four cops secured the house and Shachar and I searched the house thoroughly.

Shachar likes to search the ordinary places. It always works. Under the sofa cushions, he found brass knuckles and a combat knife.

I went to search the bedroom. I decided to adhere to Shachar's search technique and examined the self-evident places first.

I lifted the pillows on the bed. I could not see anything underneath. I reached under the heavy mattress and moved my hand slowly. Just before I finished moving my hand around the bed frame, a second before thinking how things were never simple, I felt a metal object. I braced my arms and lifted the mattress carefully.

I saw a gun.

"Shachar!" I cried out joyfully. "I've found a gun! Come and give me a hand."

Shachar came over running and took the weight of the mattress. The moment I took out the gun and examined it, my excitement was replaced with disappointment. It was a Glock with a short caliber. Our suspect had used a longer, 9 mm caliber.

"We'll just have to keep searching," said Shachar regretfully.

I agreed and looked wearily in the direction of the closet packed with clothes. There was no choice. I would have to take over that wardrobe, which, to the best of my memory, was the only one I had ever seen that was even messier than mine.

My booty, after forty minutes, consisted of two envelopes containing tens of thousands of Shekels, a steel knuckleduster and two combat knives.

Shachar finished up in the living room, the kitchen and the bathroom space. He found two more knives. The sought-after gun was not found.

Shachar sat down on the sofa and sighed. I sat down next to him and joined in the moaning.

"What a letdown!" Shachar said wearily.

"Entirely. If the gun isn't here, the chance of us finding it is close to zero,"

"Shall I call in the dog squad?"

"Sure, let them search the surroundings; perhaps he buried it somewhere nearby."

"I hope so."

"Shall we go?"

"Let's go."

But we did not leave. We were too tired. In front of us, on the television screen, the screensaver for some computer game was bouncing from one corner to another. Shachar's gaze was hypnotized by the floating logo. Suddenly he got up, took one of the remotes and started pressing buttons. Various menus appeared on the screen. Shachar was crazy for computer games. Though I had no idea if the equipment in this house was worth a lot, I understood from the sparkle in Shachar's eyes that Nagusto was a connoisseur in the field.

"Shachar, this isn't the time -" I began wearily.

"Wait a minute. There's something strange here."

Shachar switched the television input over to satellite.

"Bingo!" he jumped up and reached for the converter.

"I don't understand. What have you found?"

"I knew there were too many boxes here," he said and extracted one from the shelf under the television screen.

"I knew it!" he screamed gleefully and explained. "When the box can be extracted that easily, without having to disconnect any wires, it's easy to tell that it's just a box, that it's not connected to anything."

"I don't understand," I stared at him blankly. This specific technological field was a riddle to me.

"Never mind," he said and laid the phony electronic box on the table.

"Do you need a screwdriver?"

"I don't know... I don't think so." He pulled out a small Swiss pocket knife and opened the top of the box easily. Inside the box was a Glock model 17C with a long, 9 mm caliber.

CHAPTER 14

Sunday, June 26, 2011

"Am I allowed to know where you are?" my mother barked into my ear.

"At home." I played dumb. I knew very well what she was driving at. "That is, I'm already on my way out... in a couple of minutes."

"Where were you all Saturday?"

"Asleep."

"You slept for twenty-four hours non-stop?"

"No -" I tried to answer, but she had already pressed on. "And even if you did, when you finally got up, didn't see you all the messages I sent you? And the missed calls? Didn't you think it was worthwhile contacting your poor mother, who might be worried about you?"

In fact, I had not looked at my cell phone at all. "It's now barely seven a.m., Mom. I was thinking of calling you later," I lied.

"Let's say I believe you," she sighed. "The important thing is that all's well with you."

"Yes, all's well with me," I answered, and felt eleven years old again.

"Then can you explain to me why we didn't see you on

Friday for dinner, or on Saturday for lunch, and why you couldn't call when Shabbat was over?"

"I told you I wasn't sure I could come because I was in the middle of an ongoing investigation and I might have to work over the weekend. And that's exactly what happened. I worked Friday straight through Saturday morning. When I came home, I was so tired I fell asleep until just now. I woke up about an hour-and-a-half ago, showered, ate, walked Tsumi, and now I intend to go to work."

"Anyone would think you're the only policewoman in the Israel Police force."

"Believe me, I'm not the only one working like that." It was partially true. There were other cops, like Shachar, who were hooked, like me, but there were quite a few cops who had rightfully earned the police their bad reputation. Simple investigations dragged along because of laziness and lack of motivation. There was an excessive use of bureaucracy to create the false impression of hard work. Rather than investigate and examine the facts, cops utilized excessive and unnecessary authoritarianism. Alon had somehow managed to find people like Shachar and me, who loved their profession, and, indeed, wanted to be cops. We did not care which one of us was working more shifts or fewer shifts, and we didn't bother analyzing our pay slips. We regarded our work as our calling.

"Well, my sweet, you know I'm very proud of you. I'm simply worried. You don't work at a regular job -"

"And I also don't have a regular mother," I added and she laughed.

"All mothers are like me," she continued to laugh. "If you were a mother, you'd know what I'm talking about."

I knew she no longer said it as a reproach, so I did not

bother to answer, particularly because, in my line of work, I had encountered more than one mother who did not live up to the standards set up by my mother.

I arrived at the police station. The atmosphere was relatively sleepy. The week had just started. Nagusto had been transferred to the Detention Center at Abu Kabir and the gun sent to the lab for examination. I expected to receive quite a few answers that day. I turned on my computer. To my great surprise, an email from the lab was waiting for me. What great service!

The gun that Shachar had found in the phony converter was definitely the gun used at the Zelda Café. Furthermore, the bullets that remained in the cartridge were of the same manufacturing series as the ones that had been fired in the incident. It was strong, solid evidence. We had found the murderer.

I called Abu Kabir and asked them to send over the detainee for interrogation. An hour later, I was sitting facing him in the interrogation room. He was wearing the detention outfit the jailers gave to those who do not have an extra set of clothes. There are very few people who look good in this kind of outfit, but Nagusto was one of them. I had the feeling that he was the type of man who would look like a million dollars wearing a jute sack.

"Good morning," I smiled at him and straightened the binder laid in front of me. "I don't know if I had a chance to introduce myself properly. My name is Hadas Levinger and I'm an investigator in the Israel Police."

He looked at me without blinking.

"When we arrested you, we explained the reason for your detention. But I'll ask you anyway; do you know why you've been detained?

He continued to look at me with a hollow gaze.

"Nagusto, is anything unclear?"

"Me not speak Hebrew," he answered in broken English.

"Nagusto," I shifted to a far less pleasant tone, "if this is the game you want to play, no problem. I'll waste another half a day finding a Tigrinian interpreter, and then we'll sit here with an interpreter who'll translate for you what you understand just as well. What a shame. I don't like such games. I know that you speak Hebrew and that you understand every word that comes out of my mouth. Since I detest playing games that much, I'll tell you that we found the gun you hid in the television converter."

"Is it illegal to keep a weapon for self-defense?" he answered in flawless Hebrew. "You've seen where I live. There's plenty of crime there."

"It's definitely illegal if you don't have a permit to keep a weapon. And as far as I know, you don't have such a permit."

"I didn't know that."

"Well, then, now you know. Since your Hebrew came back so fast, I'll let you in on something else. If we find slugs at a crime scene, we can find out quite easily if the bullets were shot from a particular gun. It's just like leaving fingerprints. Amazing, isn't it!"

He resumed looking at me motionlessly. I assumed he understood very well what I was saying. I decided to change tack.

"Allow me to compliment you on your excellent Hebrew."

"Thank you."

"How many years have you been in this country, to acquire such good Hebrew?"

"About six years."

"That is..." I said and studied his documents, "... you

arrived in Israel when you were seventeen."

"Correct."

"That explains your good Hebrew. Young people absorb a language far better than adults."

He shrugged. I tried to break the ice from a different direction.

"You know, my grandfather immigrated to Israel at the age of forty-two. He never absorbed the language completely. After all, he'd been in the Nazi concentration camps and had experienced a difficult trauma."

"I know about the Holocaust."

"Very good. Did you learn about it in Eritrea?"

"No, I heard about it here because of Holocaust Memorial Day."

"They don't teach about World War II in the schools in Eritrea?"

"I didn't go to school that much."

"Because of the war?"

He nodded.

"I went over your documents and saw that you have a temporary resident status. It's a status which very few Eritreans receive. I assume you have an exceptional story indeed. Perhaps you want to tell it to me?"

He was silent.

"Perhaps it will help me understand why we found so many self-defense weapons in your apartment." I tried to entice him to open up to me. "Do you still feel threatened because of your past?"

"I don't feel like talking about my past," he grumbled. "I already sat down with enough psychologists who've tried to understand me."

"I'm not a psychologist."

"But you're also trying to understand me, aren't you?"

"Perhaps."

"Let's just say that, by the age of ten, I'd been through more than other people go through their entire life."

"I've no doubt."

"I saw my father, mother and brothers die when I was eight," he said, and took a deep breath.

"Not something an eight-year-old boy should see," I agreed.

"No." He shook his head and rubbed his right eye. Was the tough criminal beginning to soften up?

"I'm genuinely sorry for you. I understand you arrived in Israel with your uncle?"

"Yes, my mother's brother. My mother was ten years older than him and raised him like her own son. So when she was murdered and I had nowhere to go, he adopted me."

"Very nice."

"He and my aunt are good people. They came here because of me."

"What does that mean?"

"Because of the long war with Ethiopia, they kept on drafting men, women and even children, even after the war was over. My uncle had been drafted and discharged already, but he didn't want me to be drafted as well."

"How old were you?"

"Less than fifteen."

"Wow!"

"I was told to transfer to study in SAWA."

"What's that?"

"It's a military camp. My uncle wouldn't hear of it because he didn't want me to be a soldier and also because our neighbor's daughter had been kidnapped by soldiers from there. They demanded ransom money for her."

"And did they manage to get her back?"

"No. Her parents tried to get the money, but didn't succeed."

"And what happened to her?"

"After an entire village had raped her, she was sold to some Bedouin and since then, nobody knows what happened to her."

"Sad."

"Yes," he said and took another deep breath.

"So you escaped from Eritrea to Israel?"

"We went to Egypt first, but it was hard over there. There was no work and we weren't treated well because we were Christians. So my uncle paid a Bedouin who helped us cross the Sinai to get to Israel."

"And how did you receive the temporary resident status?"

"A matter of luck. I think it was because we were among the first to come. Besides, because my parents and brothers had been murdered during the war, I was recognized as a refugee."

Nagusto's frozen gaze had melted completely. I kept silent, letting him commune with his memories. It was the first time I had interrogated someone from Eritrea. I had seen quite a few Eritreans in the detention cells, but I'd never had the opportunity to speak with any of them. They were usually involved in misdemeanors and petty crime.

Nagusto's hard testimony opened a window for me onto the difficulties encountered by those who live in the margins of Israeli society. Nevertheless, the difficulties could not absolve Nagusto of his violent actions. He murdered Koby and destroyed an innocent young woman along the way. My late grandfather had been a Holocaust survivor, like his younger brother. They had gone through hell no less than Nagusto, but they chose to rebuild their lives honestly rather than take the route of crime.

"Nagusto," I said gently, "it really pains me to hear what you went through, and I'm glad that you and your uncles found refuge in Israel. You seem like a smart guy who certainly knows that not knowing the law does not exempt you from punishment. Some of the weapons we found in your apartment don't require a permit, but guns are a different story altogether. Apart from the felony of keeping guns without a permit, let me tell you that the gun we found in your apartment, the one you admitted you had for self-defense, is the gun used by the shooter in the murder at Zelda Café two weeks ago."

He looked surprised. I had to admit that his acting skills were not too bad. "I've no idea what you're talking about."

"Really?"

"Really."

"You didn't hear about the murder at Zelda Café on Monday two weeks ago? Two civilians were murdered. A motorcyclist shot them."

"Could be I saw something on television."

I bent down toward the evidence box, pulled out the hidden gun, put it on the desk and pushed it toward Nagusto.

"Does this gun look familiar?"

He bent forward toward the gun.

"No!" he said resolutely and stood up. "I've no idea where this gun is from. I know the Israel Police. You planted this gun in my apartment. And if it was not you, then somebody else had it planted in my apartment."

"Well, really," I sighed, "you're not serious. Sit down. Your fingerprints are on the gun."

I lied. The gun was clean.

His resolute look changed, and he sat down. I saw some concern in his eyes. "It can't be," he said, and for the first time I heard his pronounced accent.

"What do you mean, it can't be?" I hoped to trap him.

"I don't know. Perhaps you made a mistake in your examination," he said with confidence.

"Regretfully for you, we don't make such mistakes. I imagine you speak with such confidence because you took care to wipe the gun, and as we know, you had gloves on during the shooting. But maybe you weren't thorough enough. Maybe you touched it when you were cleaning it, maybe when you were hiding it inside the false box— I don't know. You made a mistake, Nagusto. And now you can't say it's not your gun."

"Suppose the gun's mine - it doesn't mean I fired it."

"Theoretically, you're right, of course. You were smart and took care not to remove your helmet during the shooting. I won't lie to you. We don't have an eye witness who can identify you in a lineup."

Nagusto smiled a wide smile, which exposed two rows of shiny teeth. I allowed him to enjoy the feeling of accomplishment for a moment until I went on the offensive again. "But I have quite a few witnesses who'll confirm that whoever shot Koby Ozri and Shirley Navon was riding a motorcycle identical to the one you ride. Adding the fact that, of all the places in the world, the gun used in the shooting was found in your apartment, I think - how can I put it - that it will be very hard for you to convince me and the courts that you had no connection to the murder."

"It's circumstantial," he answered. I smiled inwardly. The suspect had already managed to meet with a lawyer and had been coached well. "Somebody's trying to incriminate me."

"You don't say," I said in apparent contempt. "I'll be glad to hear who, in your opinion, is trying to incriminate you. Please direct me to the real shooter."

"I've no idea," he said, folding his arms and leaning back. "I'll tell you why you don't know. You don't know who's incriminating you because *nobody* is incriminating you. I'll tell you something else, young man. Your lawyer explained to you very nicely what circumstantial evidence is, but he's not familiar with all the evidence we have. I'll let you in on a secret: we have a witness who ties you directly to the crime scene."

Nagusto straightened up immediately.

"And I'll tell you something else that may convince you to stop playing games. I checked with the Ministry of the Interior, and your visitor visa is temporary. Indeed, it's renewed automatically every three years, but I can have it annulled in a minute, in one phone call. The fact that you're a suspect in a criminal case and my warm recommendation are sufficient for your visa to be annulled. I don't even need an indictment for Immigration to buy you a one-way airline ticket to Asmara. Believe me, it's really the last thing I want to do, but the State of Israel can't allow you to continue living here, not when you're under such severe suspicion."

The gloves were completely removed. Nagusto would cooperate with me. I was almost certain of that.

"Let's say I know something about that shooting you're talking about... why is it worth my while to talk to you about it at all? If you charge me with murder, you'll throw me in jail or out of the country either way."

He was right. I was also right in my tactic.

"Well, as I said before, you're a smart guy. So even though we started off on the wrong foot, I'm willing to forget it and make a deal with you. Do you want to hear it?"

He sighed. I interpreted it as agreement and continued. "There are three things I'm certain about: one - you killed Koby Ozri and Shirley Navon; two - someone sent you to murder them; three - you'd rather molder in an Israeli jail for twenty years than return to Eritrea. That's why I've an offer for you that you'll find difficult to refuse." He was silent. I continued in a much softer tone. "Between us, I'm a lot more interested to know who sent you. If you tell me who sent you to murder Koby Ozri, you'll do a lot less time than you otherwise will."

"And then you'll deport me?"

"I can't know what'll happen after you're released from jail. But if you behave well in jail and earn good reports, we won't recommend deporting you."

"Which means I'll have to go to jail and, in the end, you may still deport me back to Eritrea?"

"Think about the alternative."

"Which is?"

"You'll spend a lot of time and money on lawyers. There'll be a lengthy trial that will undoubtedly end with your conviction. There's sufficient evidence tying you to the incident, and there's testimony against you. Without my support, the verdict will be, at best, a life sentence in Israel followed by deportation to Eritrea, and, in the worst case, a life sentence in Eritrea."

He looked at me, shocked, trying to process the information.

"You don't have to answer me now," I told him. "I'll contact Public Defense and ask them to send you a lawyer to explain the deal and all its implications."

"Let it be," he said in a feeble voice.

"Do you want someone specific?"

"Yes. The guy I saw yesterday was nice. His name was Shuky. I don't remember his last name."

"Attorney Shuky Ben-Haim?"

"Right," he smiled with relief, "that's his name."

It was not because Shuky Ben-Haim was such a renowned lawyer that Nagusto smiled. He was one of the few Public Defense lawyers willing to be called in on weekends. This was why I remembered his name.

Monday, June 27, 2011

The plea bargain with Nagusto was signed at noon. It was one of the fastest plea bargains ever signed by the District Attorney's office. I had to admit to myself that Nagusto did not receive the best deal he could have gotten, but it did not bother me particularly. The previous evening, after the interrogation, I started digging on the internet and read scores of testimonies by refugees from Africa, mainly from Sudan and Eritrea. The stories were horrible and reminded me of the stories I had heard from my grandfather about Nazi concentration camps. I read about other people who had arrived in the country under the guise of refugees in order to get higher standards of living than they had in Africa. Those who could not get a visitor visa roamed the slums of South Tel-Aviv aimlessly, terrorizing the residents. I thought about what Nagusto had told me and wondered if his difficult story had indeed occurred, or if he had fabricated the whole thing in order to be granted a visa. My gut feeling told me that, though he was a tough criminal, he had been telling the truth. Nevertheless, that nagging doubt made it easier for me when I had to interrogate him again, knowing that he had signed a bad deal. Besides, he had murdered Koby. Let him pay.

Nagusto entered the interrogation room. I followed him in, sat down slowly and smiled at him amiably.

"Then we're past the stage where you don't know whose gun it is and how it's connected to the murder at Zelda's," I said pleasantly.

"Right."

"So, tell me, please, in your own words, what exactly you were doing on Monday, June 13, 2011 at 12:30 p.m."

He spoke dryly. "I arrived on my motorcycle in Lincoln Street in Tel-Aviv. I stopped in front of Zelda Café. I got off the motorcycle and walked toward the restaurant. When I identified my targets, I shot at them and eliminated them with the gun you found in my apartment."

"You mean target," I corrected him.

"What?" he looked at me, confused.

"The fact that there were ultimately two victims does not mean that there was more than one target. You were sent to eliminate the criminal, Koby Ozri, right?"

"No," he shook his head. "I had two targets: the guy and the girl. Between the two of them, it was more important that I eliminate the girl."

CHAPTER 15

I stormed out of the interrogation room and ran to Alon's office. The looks on Alon's and Shachar's faces said it all. Something odd was happening in this case. The innocent bystander was not as innocent as we had thought. Nagusto's testimony corresponded to Yoav Gottlieb's puzzling testimony; the hit had been aimed at Shirley. What secrets did young Shirley Navon have?

"Do you have anything to say before I continue with him?" I asked Alon.

"Levinger, remember this date."

"Why?"

"Because this is the day I was struck speechless..."

I smiled and returned to the interrogation room.

"So the girl - that is, Shirley Navon - was your main target, and Koby Ozri was your secondary target?"

"Yes."

"What exactly you were asked to do?"

"Eliminate the girl and injure Koby. That's why I had to shoot her right away, to make sure she didn't have time to hide."

"Did you know Koby or Shirley before arriving at the scene?"

"No."

"Then how did you identify them?"

"I saw pictures of them. And before leaving to go there, I got a call that confirmed they would be there. The caller described to me exactly where they would be."

"And you're sure you didn't make a mistake?"

"Hundred percent. I got the money."

"From whom?"

"No idea. I was told to go to a certain location. The money was waiting for me there in a black washbag.

"Where?"

"The Summit Garden in Jaffa."

"Fine. Let's go back a little. Tell me about the first time you were contacted about this job."

"About two weeks earlier. I'd already done a small job for this person. He contacted me and asked to meet."

"Who?"

"I don't know him. He said his name was Lior."

"Lior what?"

"I'm not even sure his name was Lior, so I certainly don't know his last name. It was all very secretive. He didn't even give me his phone number."

"Then how did you speak?"

"He was the one who made contact, and always from an unlisted number. We set up a meeting, and he told me he needed Shirley eliminated and Koby injured. He gave me the gun and showed me their pictures and asked me to remember what they looked like. He wanted the operation carried out within a few days, and that he'd take care that both of them would be in the same place at the same time."

"Do you have any idea how he took care of that?"

"I didn't ask unnecessary questions."

"How much did he pay you?"

"Two thousand shekels right there, and another ten

thousand after the hit, but since I took out Koby as well, I only got seven thousand."

The foreign workers had brought down the list price for human life. I knew from previous interrogations that the list price for a hit had once been at least three times as much.

"How did you know where to go, and when?"

"Lior called me the day before and gave me the exact details."

It was probably the phone call that Itzik Levayev had heard.

I brought all the station's picture albums to the room and asked Nagusto to identify Lior. Nagusto leafed through the hundreds of pictures, for hours. It must be said, the guy cooperated fully. However, he did not find a picture of his operator. I released him back to Abu Kabir and started to work my brain.

It was clear now that Shirley had been the main target, not Koby. However, whoever ordered the hit had known Koby as well. Furthermore, Nagusto had already conducted a "small job" for him, and he had taken care to contact him confidentially. All the signs indicated that the client was associated with organized crime. What could possibly connect Shirley Navon, a bright student and a good worker, to organized crime? Was her family connected to organized crime? I recalled Moshe Navon's rage about his perception of police incompetence. Was it a charade? It was time for a new line of interrogation.

Shirley had been engaged to a guy named Yoni, a medical student. I found his phone number among the papers I had kept from the conversation with Shirley's parents.

"Hello?" he answered with all the suspicion of someone answering an unrecognized number.

"Am I speaking with Yoni Shapira?"

"Yes. Who am I speaking with?"

"Hadas Levinger, Israel Police. I'm calling in connection with your fiancée's murder."

"What?" he sounded confused.

"First of all, I wanted to ask how you are."

"How am I?" he sighed. "Lousy... that's the truth."

"I'm really sorry to hear that."

We were silent for a moment.

"I'd like to set up a meeting with you, if possible, here at the station." I broke the silence.

"Why?"

"It's just regular procedure with the families of the victims of criminal incidents. Since the two of you lived together, I'm certain you can enlighten us."

"What's there to enlighten you about? She was simply in the wrong place at the wrong time."

"This is definitely the direction of the investigation," I lied. "Nevertheless, we must rule out any other possibilities. Besides, as I said, it's entirely routine."

"And you've only now remembered it?"

"I really apologize. We've been under enormous pressure, which is why we haven't gotten to you earlier. There's a small breakthrough in the investigation. In my opinion, you'll want to hear it."

He was silent for a moment, then said, "I have a gigantic exam tomorrow at noon. Let's set it up for Wednesday."

"Can you make it tomorrow, after the exam?"

"Is it that urgent?"

"I've already set up a meeting with someone else on Wednesday." I lied again. "It's better to get it done."

"Fine. But it'll have to be late. The exam starts at noon, and it's long."

"When can you get here?"

"Around seven."

The next stop in the new line of investigation was the Panda Cellular Company, Shirley's workplace. I entered the building, which strove to convey a state-of-the-art, high-tech ambiance. I had not set up a meeting with anybody in the company. I wanted to gauge the employees' reactions to my unexpected visit. The first to be surprised was, of course, the receptionist. She stared at my police badge as if I had laid a bomb in front of her and asked her to defuse it. After a few moments, she came to her senses and said she would call Human Resources. Several minutes later, a woman in a suit arrived in the reception area and invited me to go upstairs with her to the Administration floor. We entered a small conference room and she asked me to wait. I used the time to look around. It was obvious that a lot of thought had gone into the room's design. The furniture had clean lines and the lampshades above the long table were yellow, the color of the company's logo.

While I was grading Panda's interior designers, a pretty, fortyish woman entered the room. She smiled heartily and handed me a good quality, yellow business card.

It read: Orna Chen, Vice President of Human Resources and Administration.

I scrutinized the depths of my handbag till I found the small holder that held my business cards. I took out a crumpled card and handed it to her.

"Hadas," she said. "How can I help you?"

"I'm here in connection with the death of Shirley Navon."

"A terrible thing...."

"Absolutely."

"I don't know if you heard about it, but Panda intends to

establish a fund in her name for youths at risk."

"That's commendable."

"This terrible case has shaken up the entire company here. We've decided to try to tackle the root of the problem, and help youths at risk before they enter the cycle of crime."

"It's a great idea."

"Thank you. It won't bring Shirley back to us, but it'll give us a sense of doing something."

"Did you know Shirley personally?"

She smiled, embarrassed. "Look, here at Panda headquarters, we have about 250 employees. Of course, I don't know everybody, but I definitely remember Shirley's face."

"In which department did she work?"

"Finance."

"Can you be a little more specific? It must be quite a big department."

"Right - forty employees. At the top, there's the C.F.O.. Under him there are five controllers, and, under each controller, there are a number of people as needed. There's the Payroll Controller, Customer Relations Controller, Supplier Relations Controller, a controller in charge of contact with the banks, and a controller in charge of the financial reports and the Stock Exchange reports."

"And where did Shirley work within that structure?"

"She was under the Suppliers Section."

"What did she do there, exactly?"

"You'll have to ask those who worked with her. I'm not that much of an expert. I can only tell you that she started here about ten months ago, and those in charge of her were very satisfied with her work. Her death was a shock for everybody."

"I'm sure. Losing a young employee in such a tragic manner is quite a shock."

"Right."

"I'll want to talk with the people who worked with her. Are they here today?"

"I imagine they are. May I ask why?"

"What do you mean?" I played dumb. "It concerns the murder investigation."

"I know. But as far as I understand from the media, she simply had atrociously bad luck."

"It doesn't matter what they say in the media. We examine all avenues," I said formally. Orna stared at me, her eyes wide open. "It's a part of the investigation protocol." I tried to alleviate her astonishment.

"Yes, of course," she nodded as if she knew by heart the entire investigation protocol of the Israel Police. "How do you want to do this? Do you need a special room, or will you go through the offices?"

"I must have private conversations. It's an official interrogation."

"I understand. Where do you want to start?"

"The controller who was Shirley's direct supervisor."

"No problem. Do you want me to call him to come here?"

"No. I'll go to his office. If it turns out we'd be better off here, we'll come back."

The Finance Department dominated the entire seventh floor of the building.

"Only the department personnel and authorized employees are allowed to enter this floor," explained Orna, running her company ID through a small security device at the entrance door.

The offices on the seventh floor were somewhat dull

compared with the conference room. The design was similar, but somewhat tired-looking. The people on this floor also looked different from the ones I saw on the Administration floor. If I had to define their clothing style, the first word that would come to my mind would be "comfy." People walked around in flat shoes, jeans and comfortable shirts, without unnecessary accessories. I blended in quite well, while Orna looked like a tourist. She led me to the office of Guy Ditzman - according to the sign on the door. Orna knocked gently on the closed door and opened it slightly without waiting for a response.

Two people were sitting in the room, a man and a woman. It looked like we had interrupted them in the middle of a meeting. I scrutinized them quickly. According to their attire, they did not belong on that floor. I assumed that Guy regularly attended meetings, due to his position, and therefore had to dress smartly. As for the woman, I assumed she was the representative of an important supplier.

"Guy, may I interrupt you for a few minutes?" Orna opened the door so that Guy could see me too.

"Is it important?"

"Yes."

Guy sighed and asked the woman sitting with him to get back to him later. From the tone of his voice, I now realized that she worked for him. I found it intriguing. She was very well groomed, starting with her shiny, high-heeled shoes and the dress that complimented her shapely figure, right up to her hair, which was expensively colored and styled. It seemed that not all the employees on the seventh floor were committed to the comfy dress code.

"Hi, Orna," said the woman to Orna before leaving the

room.

Orna smiled a phony smile and closed the door. She smiled at Guy with embarrassment. "I hate to admit it... remind me, please - what's her name?"

"Sigal Elad."

"Ah, she probably started working here before me, that's why I don't remember her."

"Yes. She's been here even longer than me," Guy laughed. "She started here, oh, fifteen years ago."

"Wow, almost since the company was established."

"Right."

"Remind me, what's her position?"

"She's a controller's assistant, Suppliers Section."

"She worked with Shirley Navon, didn't she?"

"Yes."

"This is exactly why we're here. Let me introduce Inspector Hadas Levinger of the Israel Police."

"Hadas is fine," I smiled.

Guy shook my hand and signaled us to sit down.

"So Hadas, how can I help you?"

"First of all, I'd like to understand Shirley's position with the company."

"So here it is. We brought Shirley in for a temporary project in mid-2010. It was because the Tax Authority had issued a regulation requiring us to set up a unified reporting system on a monthly basis, starting in January 2010. I won't get you entangled in all the specifics, but the technical implication was that we needed help to verify that all the licensed dealer numbers of our suppliers and customers were defined accurately in the system. At first, we thought we could handle the new regulation with the existing manpower, but after several inaccurate reports, we decided to hire an employee to be in charge of it. Even though we'd designated Shirley for a temporary position, we soon realized that she was an excellent employee and that was why she stayed on."

"What did she do once that project was completed?"

"She was in charge of unified reporting each month. Indeed, there wasn't as much work as there'd been at the beginning of the project, but each month there were aberrations that had to be taken care of. She knew the system better than anybody else. Moreover, she helped Shai Hakim as well as Sigal Elad - the woman who was sitting here when you came in."

"What are their responsibilities?"

"Shai is a very experienced bookkeeper, who deals mainly with receiving material from various suppliers. Sigal, who's also a bookkeeper by training, is considered a controller's assistant because of her seniority and because her work's ranked somewhat higher. She deals with adjustments and payments to suppliers."

"Is Shai here today?"

"I think so… let me check," said Guy and called the department secretary.

I took my leave of Orna, and Guy accompanied me to the offices of Shai and Sigal. Shai was sitting in an open space of six workstations. His workstation was the farthest away. When I came closer to his workstation, my attention was drawn to a large, framed picture hung on the wall attached to the workstation. It was Shirley's picture. The inscription on the picture read:

We will remember forever.
Finance Department members, the Panda Company.

Shai was a gawky guy of about thirty-five. He was engrossed in keying numbers on his calculator. Only when we were right next to him did he notice us and break away from the calculator.

"Shalom," he said, surprised.

"Shai, how are you?" asked Guy pleasantly.

"Everything's alright…" Shai said tentatively.

Guy smiled. "Don't worry, everything's alright. I'm sorry to interrupt you like this in the middle of your work - I know you're very busy, as usual, but you'll have to take a short break."

Guy looked at me. "Do you want to sit with him over here?" he whispered.

"No. I can't speak with him in this open space. We should go back to the conference room on the top floor," I whispered back.

"Do you know where the small conference room on the Administration floor is?" he asked Shai.

"Yes."

"Can you go up there for a brief meeting?"

"Concerning what?" Shai asked with concern.

"An audit by the authorities," Guy said, to my relief. I didn't want all the employees in the room to know that I was a policewoman.

"Do I need to bring anything? Issue card indexes?"

"Not at this stage," I put in. "These are general questions."

"No problem," he said in the tone of someone used to audits. "I'm just in the middle of a report. I'll be finished within half an hour, and I'll come up."

"Excellent," I said.

We went from Shai's workstation to Sigal's office.

Guy told me that most of the company's controllers' assistants shared an office with another employee or two. Sigal, however, was a very experienced and esteemed employee, which was why she had her own office. This was better - we could stay in her office.

"Where did Shirley sit?" I wondered as we approached her office.

"She worked in the open space we just left. To the best of my memory, her workstation was one of those closer to the entrance."

I asked him to show me her workstation after I was done with the round of questioning.

Sigal's office was actually a very small room. I tried to recall the size of my bathroom, and doubted if Sigal's room was much bigger.

"Sigal?" Guy knocked gently on Sigal's open door. She raised her head toward us and smiled broadly.

"Yes?" she asked with curiosity while her fingers moved skillfully over the keyboard.

"May I interrupt you for a few minutes?"

"You can always interrupt me," she answered flirtatiously.

Guy chuckled with unconcealed pleasure. "I'd like to introduce Hadas. She's from the Israel Police."

I did not notice any change in Sigal's expression. She was not surprised or scared. "Hadas needs to ask you a few questions in connection with Shirley's murder," Guy said and hurried to add, "God rest her soul."

Sigal made a face. "How come? What's our connection to the story? I thought she was an accidental victim."

"Just procedure," I said dryly and moved one of the chairs. "May I sit down?" I asked and sat down while Sigal was nodding.

"Do you need me here?" asked Guy.

"No. If you could just make sure the conference room's available and Shai gets there..."

"No problem," he said, went out and closed the door behind   him.

CHAPTER 16

"So, you're a longtime employee of Panda," I said to Sigal, who continued to type diligently.

"Yes," she said without raising her eyes from the computer. "Excuse me for a second. I have to complete this payment order. If I stop in the middle, I'll have to start over."

"Okay."

"You can talk to me," she smiled. "I'm not doing anything complicated. I can listen at the same time."

"Good. As you know, I'm investigating Shirley Navon's death. Guy told me she worked with you."

"She worked mainly with Shai Hakim, but she started working with me, too, about four months ago."

"What can you tell me about her?"

"A very smart girl. Studying accounting at the university - so sad -"

"Were the two of you close?" I cut her off.

Sigal raised her head and looked at me. "The truth is, we weren't. She was a really a lovely girl, but we were in different phases in life. She was a young student enjoying life in Tel-Aviv, while I'm a mother of four from Ramat Hasharon." I smiled at her, and she finally let out the burning question that had aroused the curiosity of every person I had met in the last hour.

"Excuse me for asking, but –"

"I assume you want to know why I'm interviewing you. As I said, it's routine procedure. In the course of a murder investigation, I need to interrogate all the people close to each victim. One can never know who was an accidental victim, and who was not," I said, and scrutinized her face. Under the layer of makeup, I noticed a look of surprise.

"You think Shirley *wasn't* an accidental victim?"

"I didn't say that. I said one can never know."

"If that's the case, it'd be the weirdest story in the world."

"Why?"

"Why would anybody want to hurt a sweet girl like Shirley?"

"I thought you didn't know her very well?"

"I knew her well enough to find it hard to believe that anything like that would happen to her."

"Okay. Let's move forward. Can you please explain to me in simple terms what Shirley did for you, exactly?"

"Did anybody explain to you the structure of our financial system?

"More or less."

"I belong to the Suppliers Section, and the crux of my duties is actually treasury management. I prepare payments to the suppliers. Since it concerns the banks, I also work with the controller in charge of working with the banks on anything associated with bank adjustments."

"It sounds complicated."

"Only for someone who doesn't understand. Believe me, it's not complicated work. The ones who complicate it are all the people in the middle."

"What does that mean?"

"The activity that ends with a payment to the supplier begins, in fact, with a user in the company. Suppose there's an engineer who needs certain components for his work. He opens up an order. The order's transferred to the Acquisitions Department. Acquisitions pass a quote from the supplier to the engineer. If the quote's approved, the Acquisition personnel order the components from the supplier. The supplier ships the components with the tax invoice for approval. After the approval, the payment's transferred to the supplier according to our terms, which are usually current plus 60 days."

"I admit I'm a little lost. Can you explain to me where the problem is?"

"The problem derives from an age-old company policy, according to which, whoever initiated the deal must approve the tax invoice. What happens in reality is that, more than once, invoices haven't been approved because it's a bureaucratic headache for a lot of employees. Worse than that, sometimes they discard the invoices because they think they're redundant paperwork. Consequently, many invoices don't get paid and don't even get recorded by the Finance Department."

"I understand. And how did Shirley fit into the picture?"

"Shirley was brought in because of the new VAT reporting regulations."

"Yes, I've heard about that."

"I asked for her help with everything related to approving invoices for payment, once the pressure was off her."

"I understand. Are there unpleasant situations with suppliers or employees?"

"None at all with the employees. Once in a while, an

employee receives a friendly reprimand for being late approving an invoice, but nothing more."

"And with the suppliers?"

"That's something else entirely. Most of the suppliers accept a slight delay in payment, but there are those who can be difficult to handle."

"Tell me more."

"There are those who yell and threaten us, others pester us on the phone dozens of times a day. There have even been some who shame us on social media."

"Are there suppliers whose threats sound violent, or who threaten to use violence?"

"I don't recall anything like that. After all, we're a reputable company. We don't do business with criminals."

"If I understand you correctly, the person who received most of those unpleasant calls over the last few months was Shirley?"

"Right."

"Were you aware of any calls involving threats?"

"No. She always informed me when she had a relatively unusual call. I'm sure that if someone were to threaten her with violence, she'd have informed me, as well as the more senior staff."

"I'd appreciate a list of all the suppliers with whom there have been payment problems recently."

"No problem," she said and wrote down a memo for herself in an open notebook beside her.

"You said you weren't particularly close."

"That's right."

"Did you ever have lunch together?"

"Rarely. I hardly ever eat lunch here. I leave early to eat with my kids." She pointed at a cork notice board covered with pictures of her with her family.

"Do you know anyone that she have lunch with?"

"She had a good girlfriend from the main secretariat, and I know they used to eat together a lot. Shai clung to them like a leech."

"What do you mean?"

Sigal smiled. "Shai was hooked on Shirley. He took advantage of any opportunity to be in her company."

"Didn't he know she was engaged to be married?"

"I assume so, but let's just say, he's a somewhat peculiar guy."

This explained the large picture above Shai's workstation, I noted to myself, and chuckled at Sigal, like a partner in office gossip. "Where did they used to eat?"

"There's a dining hall on the third floor, but not many employees eat there. The food won't be getting a Michelin star any time soon, if you know what I mean."

We smiled at each other and she continued. "That's why the employees tend to bring food from home, or get takeouts from local places. They rarely eat out. It simply takes too long."

"Did they bring in food from the Zelda Café sometimes?"

"Yes. It's quite a popular place."

"Did you eat there?"

"Sure. I've eaten there several times. Nice place. I hope they manage to get the business running again."

"I also hope so, too," I said and took my leave from her.

Shai Hakim was waiting for me in the small conference room. His leg was swaying jerkily under the desk. He looked tense.

"It'll be very difficult for me to answer questions without my computer," he said before I had even had a chance to sit down opposite him. I recalled that he was thinking that he had been summoned for an audit.

"I don't think you'll need a computer," I smiled and examined him. The description that came to my mind was "old-school nerd." He had greasy hair parted on the side, and wore old-fashioned glasses with particularly thick lenses. There were two pens in the pocket of his well-pressed shirt. I could not help peeking at his feet. His closed sandals did not surprise me. He was rather a good-looking man, but he managed to conceal it very well.

"I'm not from Income Tax or VAT," I told him. "I'm from the Israel Police."

"Is it about Shirley's murder? It's about time!"

This was an unexpected reaction.

"You're the first person I've spoken with from the company who sounds like he expects Shirley's death to be investigated," I said.

"Really?" he wondered. "I was sure you'd be here right after the murder. To my knowledge, it's a part of the interrogation procedure."

"You're right, and here I am. I understand you worked with Shirley."

"True," he said, his voice trembling.

"What can you tell me about her?"

He lowered his head. When he raised it, I noticed that his eyes were glistening.

"Shirley was -" He choked up. He closed his eyes in an attempt to hold back his tears, but they had a will of their own. "Shirley was the most amazing girl I ever met in my life."

There was a stack of napkins on the desk, probably left over from the refreshments from a meeting. I brought the stack closer to him. He pulled one out and wiped the wet lenses of his glasses.

"I understand she was very dear to you."

"Very much so. I loved her."

"You knew she was engaged?"

"Yes, I knew. But now she's not engaged to anyone," he said in an odd voice.

I felt a shudder go down my spine. "I want to know if I understand you right. Did you love her in a romantic sense?"

"I loved her in every possible sense. I don't really have a lot of experience with girls. I'm rather awkward on dates, certainly when I really like a girl."

"You didn't go out on a date with Shirley, did you? But you worked with her very closely, as I understand."

"Yes," he said wistfully. "They brought her in to help me because of the new VAT regulations."

"I know, it's been explained to me already," I hurried to say. Shai seemed to me like the type of person who would burst into a long and tiring lecture on Value Added Tax regulations and their implementation. "Let's move on. What can you tell me about your work with Shirley? Why did you love her so much?

"She wasn't like other girls," he said, biting his lip and rolling his eyes. "She was beautiful and gentle on the inside as much as on the outside. Sometimes, female interns from public accounting firms come here dressed in their tailored suits, and when they ask me questions I can see they don't understand anything. Many public accountants are unfamiliar with the work of the bookkeepers and don't understand it. But they patronize me because I'm 'just' a bookkeeper." He almost spat out the word "just" and marked imaginary quotes with his hands.

"And Shirley?"

"Shirley was also studying to be a CPA, but she treated

me with respect. She even said that she'd learned more from me than she had from her tutors at the university. She learned fast and had an excellent understanding of the work."

"Was that why you loved her that much?"

"I held her in high esteem professionally, but I loved the person she was. She understood me better than any other person, except for my mother, maybe. She was the first girl in my life I could talk to about almost any subject in the world. She knew how to listen and give excellent advice."

"And what did she feel toward you, in your opinion?"

"I know it was mutual."

"How can you be so sure?"

"A couple of months ago, my mother called me at my workstation. I wasn't there and Shirley picked it up. When Shirley heard it was my mother, she told her she was working with me, and that she had a wonderful, smart son. When I spoke with my mother later and she told me about it, she said Shirley must be in love with me. I explained to her that she was only a good friend and she was already engaged."

"How did you cope with the fact that she was engaged to someone else?"

"It was hard, I admit. I'd found the love of my life, a girl I could open up to and speak with freely, and the thought that she was going to marry another guy - who wasn't right for her at all, in my opinion - was driving me crazy! But after the conversation with my mother, I got up some courage. I waited one evening when she was staying late to make up time. When there was almost nobody left on the floor and we could talk intimately, I confessed my love to her."

"How did she react?"

"She stuttered and apologized and explained that I was very important to her and very dear, but she was engaged, so it couldn't happen. I felt she was just making excuses and it wasn't what she was really feeling. I'm no expert on relationships, but I heard how Yoni, her fiancée, talked to her and saw how he was treating her."

"How was he treating her?"

"He was a medical student. His time was more important than hers. She always had to be considerate of him because, supposedly, what he was studying was more important. After all, he was going to save lives. She was breaking her back studying and working and supporting both of them."

"It doesn't sound to me like an unusual attitude. It even makes sense. I don't suppose his studies left him time to work."

"I'm not saying otherwise, but it was his overall attitude. I saw how he offended her. He talked to her disrespectfully more than once."

"I still don't understand how you got it from her that your feelings were mutual."

"After my confession, she became very distant. It was hard for her to speak with me. I was embarrassed, too. I regretted destroying everything, because I needed her in any form or manner and her distance made it difficult. However, one evening, about a week after my confession, Yoni treated her badly again. It was her cousin's birthday party and he notified her almost at the last minute that he wouldn't be able to come, because he preferred to spend time with a friend of his who was over from London for a few days. Shirley was very hurt because she'd organized the party and had taken care that the date would fit his busy schedule. She wanted him so much to attend the party. When their conversation turned nasty, she went to an empty office down the hall to talk privately. I went over there and saw she was completely shattered. I couldn't leave her like that, so I went in and hugged her. She returned my hug, then she kissed me. I swear to you... I didn't dream it, or just hope it would happen. It was the sweetest moment in my life..."

"Shirley kissed you?" I asked, almost shouting. "On the lips?" I tried to be precise.

"Yes, a real kiss." A note of longing was woven in his voice.

"And?"

"I was very excited. I began to cry and Shirley was crying anyway. I told her right away that I loved her, but she was very confused. She said she had to think about the entire situation. Then she didn't come to work for several days. I called her and she didn't pick up, only texted me asking not to call because she needed time to think. It was a nightmare for me, but it was worth it. When she returned to the office, she accepted it."

"Explain, please," I said, making a great effort to conceal my astonishment about the odd development in his convoluted story.

"She said she realized she loved me too, and that she couldn't continue living in an unequal relationship that lacked so much respect."

"When was that?"

"A little over a month ago."

"But her family didn't know about her decision to leave Yoni. Right?"

"Right. This was one of Shirley's great qualities. She always knew how to put others before herself. She didn't want to bother Yoni during such a critical exam period, so she planned on telling him at the end of his school year."

"Which means, then, that Yoni had no idea Shirley was about to leave him."

"To the best of my knowledge, no."

CHAPTER 17

Tuesday, June 28, 2011

"Then our Shirley had a secret," said Alon. "To be fair, I must admit that this investigation keeps on springing surprises."

"Yes," I smiled. "It's definitely unusual. The problem is, I find it hard to understand how this little secret's even connected to the fact that she was the target of the hit."

"Have we never seen cases before of cheated partners who decided to settle the accounts?"

"No... But Yoni didn't know about the secret affair."

"That's what Shai thinks. Maybe Yoni found out about the affair and decided to settle the account. According to what you're telling me, he wasn't someone who'd just move on when people don't dance to his tune. You said it's been difficult to set up a meeting with him for questioning. Wouldn't you expect a supportive partner to run to the police and help as much as he could?"

"There's something in what you say..."

"I wouldn't rule out Mr. Shai himself, too."

"Shai? What's his connection? What interest would he have in killing the woman who, according to him, he loved dearly and was about to become his partner?"

"Let's not jump to conclusions. You said he was a little peculiar. We can't rule out entirely the possibility that the secret affair was the product of his feverish imagination. Maybe he realized the girl would never be his. Didn't he say something about how she wasn't engaged to anybody anymore?"

"Right," I said and recalled how this sentence had made me shiver when I heard it.

"Then maybe he decided that she shouldn't belong to anybody. And if suspicion could be thrown onto Shirley's fiancé along the way, then he'd also take his revenge on his avowed rival."

"Sorry, but this sounds delusional."

"You said the guy was weird, so I'm looking for delusional stories to fit him." Alon winked at me.

I laughed and got up. I had a lot of material to go over.

"When's the fiancé coming in for questioning?"

"He said he'd be here this evening."

"In the evening?"

"He has an exam. He's a medical student."

Alon picked up his cell and checked something. "I can't be here this evening. Update me right after you're finished."

"Sure."

Was the secret affair the product of Shai's feverish imagination? The thought reverberated in my mind.

I looked at the picture that Shirley's parents had provided to the media. Shirley was good-looking and well-educated, an outstanding student with a bright future ahead of her. It was easier to associate her with a medical student than with a dull bookkeeper. However, I was precisely the one, more than anybody else, who should know that external features do not have to be the determining factor when it comes to love. Yinon had been attracted to me even though I had never bothered to cultivate my appearance. He, in contrast, closely monitored his nutrition, physical activity and clothing. Each time my mother had reprimanded me for my atrocious appearance, claiming I should invest more effort in keeping a man like Yinon, he would take me in his arms and hug me warmly, stressing that he had been madly attracted to my brain. What was it in Shai Hakim that had possibly made Shirley fall in love with him, and want to leave Yoni, the brilliant medical student, for him?

Diving into the police and government databases for two hours revealed to me a very different man from the one I had met. Shai Hakim was thirty-four, and had a graduate degree in history and a teaching certificate. He had started teaching at a High School in Central Israel, but did not succeed in passing his probationary year, so was never accepted fully into the education system. He had worked in bookkeeping throughout his studies, so when he left teaching, he returned to the field that had financed his studies.

Shai did not have a Facebook page, so it was a little hard to find out details about his personal life and his hobbies. However, I found his name and picture on two websites associated with running marathons. With each passing moment, the secret affair of Shai and Shirley seemed to me more feasible. Shirley may have succeeded in seeing the athletic, sensitive and educated man hiding under the guise of a nerdy bookkeeper. I was eager to hear Yoni's side of the story, but there were still several hours before our meeting. So I left everything and went out for lunch.

When I returned, there was a message waiting for me, with the list of suppliers I had asked Sigal to send me.

She wrote that, to the best of her memory, those were the problematic suppliers, and that if she recalled any more, she would send them.

The list was amazingly organized and included just over thirty names of suppliers and contacts. Sigal indicated in the comments the reason for each supplier's inclusion in the list. There were those who had argued regularly over the terms of payment, and there were others who had initiated one-time confrontations because of a misunderstanding or a business dispute. It wasn't a long list, but thirty names meant thirty wearying interrogations. If the person who had ordered the hit had been one of the suppliers, why would he choose to strike at the lowest ranking person in the organization? Why not strike at one of the directors? Maybe it was a warning shot and the company directors knew well that they were next in line?

I skimmed the names on the list. I did not recognize any of them. Apparently, big companies did not enter into petty squabbles over payment terms. When I looked more thoroughly, a name caught my eye: L. Z. Engineering Services, Ltd. I entered the company's name in the database, and when its details appeared, I realized why the name was familiar. Zvika Leibovitz was the owner of a consulting mechanical engineering firm. His employees usually worked on the customer's premises rather than the company's office. One of the employees, by the name of Yinon, had worked for Zvika for five years before going to work for one of Zvika's customers. I dialed Yinon's number without thinking too much.

"Hi," he said in a whisper. "I'm in a meeting... wait just a second."

"It's alright, I can call later," I suggested, but he probably was not listening. I heard a jumble of talk in the background and Yinon's voice, apologizing.

"How are you?" he asked excitedly when his surroundings were finally quiet.

"Everything's alright. I don't like interrupting you, really. We can talk later."

"You rescued me from the longest and dullest meeting in history. As far as I'm concerned, you can speak with me now about anything you want," he said happily.

I giggled. "Okay, thanks. The truth is, it's a work-related question."

"Ha," he said, disappointed. "Well?"

"Do you remember working for Zvika Leibovitz?"

"Of course. Stingy Zvika. Who could forget?"

"Do you remember how long you worked for him?"

"Until the beginning of 2008. I left right before our trip to New Zealand. I remember I'd been accepted for the job at Indigo, and then we decided to go on our trip before I started my new job," Yinon reminded me.

I remembered. This was exactly how it had happened. Before the yearning for that distant period overwhelmed me, I hurried to ask, "Do you remember the official name of Zvika's company?"

He thought for a moment. "Z. L. Engineering," he said hesitantly.

"Is it possible that you're switching the initials? Was it L. Z. Engineering Services, Ltd.?"

"Yes, yes," he agreed immediately. "What you just said. This was the name that appeared on the pay slips."

"Did you know any people over there?"

"Why are you asking?" his curiosity was piqued.

"Hmm. It's related to my investigation. The company's name came up in relation to a business dispute with the Panda Company."

"The cellular company?"

"Yes. What's Zvika's connection to Panda? Why would Panda need to consult over an engineering matter?"

"No idea. Zvika's very well connected. It could be that they needed advice on outfitting electronic equipment, or something along those lines."

"Okay. There's no chance I'll understand what you're talking about. Let's return to the issue itself. Do you remember Zvika? Or his employees? I mean, the financial personnel in particular?"

Yinon exhaled. "Wow, it's been over three years. I'm not sure all of them would still be there."

"Zvika's certainly still there."

"Well, he's the owner."

"What's he like?"

"In my opinion, a good man, but many thought he was a chronic penny-pincher."

I remembered that the terms of Yinon's employment had met the requirements of the law to the letter without a single enhancement. He had always received his salary on the last possible day.

I returned to Sigal's list and looked at the comment she had written. According to her description, Panda had called L. Z. once, and after providing the service, the supplier had called dozens of times, harassing the department's personnel and threatening them. She did not specify what type of threats.

"Can you guess at why Zvika would harass the Panda Company and threaten them?"

"I'm almost certain I know what happened there."

"Really?"

"Yes. Zvika provided services to Panda and they didn't pay him - something like that."

"Exactly. How did you know?"

"It was Zvika's primary difficulty, working with big

companies. On one hand, they provided him with secure, good work, but some companies have terrible payment ethics."

"Big companies, too?"

"Yes. The worst to work with were the defense companies, but there was no choice. A considerable amount of work in mechanical engineering comes from the military."

"Why is that?"

"You're asking me?" Yinon chuckled. "I'm a mechanical engineer, not a finance expert. For a company like Zvika's, any delay in payment was problematic. He had to pay his employees on time, but he received the money from his customers only after a long time, with a lot of chasing and nagging. If he threatened them, it was understandable. It's definitely frustrating and unpleasant to have to chase up customers' payments."

"Was it like that with all the customers, every month?"

"That would be an exaggeration. It happened mainly with one-off projects."

Yinon's answer corresponded to Sigal's comment. I erased Zvika's company from the list of possible suspects.

"It's annoying," I said.

"Yes," answered Yinon.

A few oddly silent moments followed.

"Do you want to meet up?" asked Yinon.

It is not a question of wanting, I thought to myself. "I don't know if that's advisable," I said.

"You could come to visit Orit and me," Yinon hastened to add, offering Orit as a defensive wall against mutual loss of control. We both knew that any meeting between us was volatile. Yinon sounded desperate to see me.

"I'm in the middle of a high-pressure investigation. I

can't set up anything," I tried to get out of it.

"But we'll set something up, sometime?" he almost begged.

"Alright," I muttered. I was desperate myself.

I hung up. In a moment of candor, I admitted to myself that that conversation had not been necessary for the continuation of the investigation. I had, indeed, eliminated one name from the list, but it definitely had not been the only reason I called Yinon.

I decided to move on to a more practical inspection. I entered the business permit numbers of the suppliers to the search databases. I found that the owners of three of the companies had criminal records. Two of those had criminal records for tax evasion and false registrations in corporate documents. The third person had a criminal record for extortion. His name was Yossi Baruch. I returned to Sigal's list and found the name of the business owned by Yossi Baruch – Super-Duper. I assumed it was a supermarket that provided groceries for Panda. The comment indicated that there had recently been a misunderstanding with the customer in regard to tax invoices. The name of the business sounded very familiar. I entered the name in Google Maps. Bingo. Super-Duper was two stores away from the Zelda snack bar.

I called Sigal.

"Do you know Yossi Baruch?" I asked.

"No."

"He's the registered owner of Super-Duper."

"Ah... Yossi... Yes, sure! We do some shopping at his place, like coffee, soft drinks, cleaning materials and refreshments for guests."

"You noted that there had been some problems with him lately. What did you mean?"

"Yes. It was rather unpleasant. Usually, there are no problems with him, but apparently one of our employees didn't transfer the tax invoice to bookkeeping, and Yossi waited for his payment for a long time. It was a rather large invoice, for a lot of refreshments."

"What was unpleasant?"

"He called my office and yelled at me. It was quite unusual. Our relationship with him had been very cordial until then."

"And that was the end of the story?"

"Not really. We decided to cut down our dealings with him. His outburst was, indeed, unusual and unreasonable. We still purchase some products from him here and there, but not on credit and on a far smaller scale."

"Did you know he has a criminal record?"

"Wow, I didn't!" She sounded surprised.

"Did he have a confrontation with Shirley about it?"

"Could be. He claimed he'd delivered the tax invoice to her, but she said she hadn't received anything from him."

"You've been very helpful. Thank you."

"My pleasure. I have to go over several more suppliers. Do you want me to send you an additional list?"

"Yes, sure. Thanks again," I said and hung up.

Yossi Baruch had been released from jail in 2001 after serving a three-year sentence for extortion. He belonged to a criminal gang that had disbanded in the meantime. Following his release, he travelled to the US and returned to Israel after five years. He opened his store on Lincoln Street, and - at least, on paper - he stayed away from the world of crime. How did he finance the establishment of a new supermarket in the center of Tel-Aviv? I could only guess. I printed Yossi's picture from the Prison Service database. It was a ten-year-old picture, but it was the most up-to-date one I could obtain at this stage.

Thirty minutes later, I was waiting for Nagusto in one of the interrogation rooms at Abu Kabir. He dragged himself into the room looking weary.

"How are you?"

"Alright."

"Do you remember saying that you met with somebody who asked you to eliminate Shirley?"

"Yes."

"I'm going to show you a picture. I'm telling you in advance that this picture isn't up-to-date, but it's very clear. I want you to try to remember if this is the same Lior who asked you to eliminate Shirley and Koby."

I handed him the picture. He examined it and returned it to me after a few seconds.

"This isn't the man."

"Are you sure?" I asked, disappointed.

"One hundred percent."

"It doesn't even resemble him a little? I told you it's not up-to-date. The man in the picture's ten years older today."

"I'm positive it's not the man."

"Why?"

"The man in the picture looks older than Lior. So if it's a picture from ten years ago, then it's definitely not him."

I left Nagusto regretfully. I had hoped he would identify Yossi and the mystery would be solved.

The fact that Yossi was not the same mysterious Lior who had met with Nagusto did not rule out the possibility that he had ordered the hit. It was possible that he was the customer and Lior was his field agent. But, at this point, without Nagusto identifying him, I had no basis for an arrest warrant for Yossi. I had no choice but to drive to Super-Duper on Lincoln Street and hope that Yossi Baruch would agree to speak with me.

CHAPTER 18

I was already inside my car, ready to move off, when vigorous knocking on the window made me jump in my seat. It was one of the junior prison staff from Abu Kabir.

"Hadas Levinger?"

"Yes."

"I was asked to call you back to the interrogation room. It's urgent!"

My heart leapt. I turned off the engine and almost ran back to the interrogation room.

Nagusto was sitting there, holding a copy of *Israel Today*. I sat down opposite him, and before I could ask why he had called me back, he burst into an explanation.

"After you left, they took me back to my cell. I asked to stop for a second at the water cooler for a drink. While I was drinking, the jailer picked up this paper from one of the chairs." He brandished the paper in his hand. "As we continued on to the cell, I noticed Lior's picture in the paper. I immediately had them call you back."

I looked at him, alert. He turned the paper to the back page, to the gossip section.

"Here." He pointed at one of the pictures. "This is Lior - the one in the white shirt."

I took the paper from him. It was a picture from the launch of some product.

The picture showed two guys and a girl laughing in a phony way at the camera. I did not recognize the girl, but, according to the caption, she had been a participant in a reality show. I did not recognize Lior, the guy in the white shirt, either. But I knew very well who the tall, muscular guy in the black shirt was.

It was Tom Sela, who, only two weeks earlier, had been sitting across from me in the interrogation room. He had been smiling a lot less, then, of course.

I was satisfied. Nagusto also looked satisfied with his fortuitous identification. I studied the picture of the egotistical duo and my smile vanished. It was the word of an Eritrean refugee threatened with deportation against the word of two *Sabras*, one of them, at least outwardly, the salt of the earth. A connecting link was missing.

"Are you positive Lior never called you from an identifiable phone?" I asked hopefully.

"No, he was really scrupulous."

"And he paid you in cash?"

"Yes."

"How? In an envelope? In rolled bills?"

"He gave me the advance in rolled bills, but the rest was in a kind of black washbag."

"What did you do with the bag?"

"I don't remember. I think I kept it in the closet. I thought I'd use it for travelling."

I thanked Nagusto, took the newspaper and rushed to the police station.

I went straight to Alon's office and showed him the picture. He recognized the guy and provided me with complete details. Lior Zemach was his complete and real name, and he was Yaakov Sela's nephew. Lior's family kept its distance from the Sela family, but they lived in the same city. Lior and Tom had attended the same school, where they became good friends. Lior had been attracted to the Sela family's life of luxury and, consequently, they were quite happy to draw him into their dubious business. Unlike Tom, who completed his full military service, Lior was discharged after one year due to incompatibility. His first criminal indictment was submitted several months later, though his criminal record was relatively scanty - marginal felonies with no genuine public interest. The arrests and interrogations were designed to wear down the Sela family and gain access the higher echelons of their hierarchy. I had not yet had a chance to interrogate him.

That was about to change.

I dispatched a police car with two cops, instructing them to turn Nagusto's apartment inside out until they find the black washbag. An hour later, the bag was with Forensics and I was on my way with two police cars and six patrolmen to Yaakov Sela's supermarket chain's headquarters. The offices were located above the company warehouse. I directed one police car to block the exit from the parking lot, and another cop was sent to the back exit to make sure that nobody escaped that way. The receptionist on the ground floor was far from surprised to see a bunch of cops. Apparently, she was used to it. Without fuss, she stood up and demanded to see a warrant. I showed her the arrest warrants and she fell silent. I did not pressure her. After a few moments, she pointed at the stairs.

"They're in the office upstairs," she said quietly and sank back into her armchair. I left her with one cop and went upstairs with the three remaining cops.

As soon as we entered the space of the upper floor, I identified Lior and Tom. They were sitting with three other men in a conference room partitioned by glass walls. I went toward the glass door, but suddenly heard an imposing female voice.

"Excuse me. Who are you looking for?"

I turned and saw the speaker. She was a good-looking young woman, sitting at a side desk at the entrance to the floor, holding a phone receiver. I was so focused on Lior and Tom that I had not noticed her before.

The woman put down the receiver, got up and approached me.

"As you've just been informed by the receptionist," I said and pointed at the telephone lying on the woman's desk, "I need to speak with Tom and Lior."

She smiled like someone who just heard a really humorless joke. "You'll have to wait," she said, and folded her arms.

I pulled out the two warrants. "I'm really not waiting," I said. I signaled to the cops to stay with her and stormed into the conference room. The eyes of all present were directed toward me. Tom and Lior got up together and looked at me menacingly. Within two seconds, they noticed the uniformed cops standing outside and their look was transformed. Tom needed a few additional seconds to recognize me and put on an innocent expression.

"Hello, everybody," I said in my most authoritative tone. "Sorry for the interruption. I am Inspector Hadas Levinger, from the Tel-Aviv Police. Tom Sela and Lior Zemach, you're under arrest. Put your hands up, please. The rest of you, put your hands on the desk."

They obeyed silently. The cops entered the conference room and handcuffed Tom and Lior. A crowd started to assemble outside the conference room as the employees came out of their offices to watch. I assumed it was not the first time they had seen their bosses being arrested.

"Return to your offices!" I commanded. "The show's over!" I pulled out my radio and informed the entire team that the suspects had been apprehended and they should wait for me together.

"I don't understand," Tom said almost tearfully as we were going down the stairs, "I already told you everything I know two weeks ago…"

Lior preferred to stay silent.

When we arrived downstairs, I read the suspects their rights. I instructed the cops to send Tom in one police car, and got into the second car with Lior. I assumed he would remain silent, but I wanted to examine his body language. As expected, he projected tension.

When we arrived at the station, Tom yelled at me, "Inspector Levinger! Inspector Levinger!" I approached him.

"I'm telling you again," he said, now with real tears. "It's a mistake, you're arresting the wrong person! It's simply an outrage! You've conspired against me because I'm Yaakov Sela's son. When my father hears about it, he'll sue the police and you'll all have to look for another job."

Lior was standing next to me. He closed his eyes, bit his lower lip and signaled to Tom with a small shake of his head to shut him up. Had his hands been free, I assume he would have jumped on Tom in order to silence him. But Tom did not notice Lior's subtle signal and kept up his torrent of condemnations and threats all the way to the cells.

My phone vibrated. It was Shachar, letting me know that Yaakov Sela had been arrested as well, and they were on their way to the station. Things had finally begun to roll! I went to my room to go over the material before I started interrogating the wider Sela family. I had barely sat down when a raucous knock on the door cut off the brief silence.

It was Ricky. She peeked inside and asked cautiously, "May I interrupt you?"

"Not really," I said impatiently. "I'm under insane pressure..."

"I know," she said and slipped carefully into my office, careful to close the door behind her. "There's someone here claiming you told him to come in for questioning. He's driving me crazy!"

"What? Who is it?"

"Some Yoni. A really, really unpleasant guy!"

"Wow, right!" I pressed my hands to my forehead. It was Shirley Navon's fiancé, presenting himself for questioning. How could I have forgotten about him?

"See if he can wait for me for about an hour."

She laughed sarcastically. "He's already been waiting for you for an hour. I'd like to see you convince him to wait even one more minute..."

CHAPTER 19

Yoni looked furious.

"Thanks for coming in," I said in an attempt to cool his anger a little. "I remember you told me you're in the middle of exams."

"Right," he said, not at all mollified by my reconciliatory attempt. "That's why I don't understand why you couldn't notify me that there was such a long delay. Every minute's important to me."

"I apologize, but the nature of my work is such that an unexpected event can happen at any given moment, and then all my appointments are necessarily postponed or cancelled."

"So I see. I just don't understand why it's so difficult to update someone who already has an appointment with you."

"You're right," I said in my softest tone. "It would have been appropriate to contact you and let you know. It was a mistake not to. We're human after all."

He made a face. I could not figure out if my apology had been accepted. Perhaps he had detected that it was not genuine.

"I don't understand why it's necessary to interrogate me at all."

"I'm not interrogating you. I just need to ask you a few questions -"

"Whatever..."

"Listen, Shirley was murdered. We have to examine all the possibilities."

"What possibilities can there be?"

"She worked with money, dealt with many suppliers..."

"For Panda!" he almost shouted. "Not a front for the mafia!"

"Criminal elements can be found in all sectors of society. Did you know that one of the suppliers she worked with had served time for extortion and threats?"

"What?" He looked shocked.

"Then you didn't know."

"No. I didn't!"

"Shirley didn't tell you about her work?"

"Not much."

"Why? You were living together..."

"We didn't have time for long conversations after she started working. Each one of us was busy with their own affairs."

"So she didn't keep you in the picture about what was happening with her work? You didn't hear from her about the suppliers she was working with? Or her co-workers?"

"She mentioned several people once in a while. I admit I didn't pay attention to the details."

"Who do you remember?"

"A girl named Ella. I think she was a secretary and they used to have lunch together. I remember her because they used to socialize after work as well, so I bumped into her several times."

"Who else?"

"There was Shai the Weirdo."

"Shai the Weirdo?"

"Yes," he smiled. "That was what she called him."

"Why?"

"I don't know. I assume because he was… well, weird. I didn't meet him, but that was what she said about him."

"Did she tell you anything else about him?"

"Not too much. She only talked about him when she first started working at Panda. She said he was really a good employee and she was learning a lot from him, but he fitted the popular image of a bookkeeper."

"Do you know anyone she worked with recently?"

"I think she said she was working with someone more senior called Einav."

"Are you sure her name was Einav?"

"No."

"Could it be Sigal?"

"Yes!" he smiled and nodded. "Sigal!"

"What can you tell me about Sigal?"

"Nothing. I told you already. We didn't have much time to sit and talk."

"Okay," I said and looked at him directly. I knew the next question would upset his complacency. "How would you describe your relationship with Shirley?"

"What do you mean?"

"How was your relationship? Good? Tense? Had you quarreled much recently?"

The anger erupted in his eyes again. "I thought this wasn't an interrogation!"

"It isn't."

"Then what's this question about? Why does the quality of my relationship with Shirley matter? Am I a suspect?"

"Absolutely not."

"Then I really don't understand what you're asking."

"I asked a simple question and I'd like an answer."

He took a deep breath, thought for a long moment, and said, "Even though I've no idea why you're asking, I will answer, because I really have nothing to hide. My relationship with Shirley was very good. I wouldn't say the sparks we had at the beginning of our relationship were still firing up, but I loved her a lot. We were going to get married!"

"According to what you're saying, it sounds like you were drifting apart. You didn't talk very much -"

"Right, but only because we were busy with our studies."

"But Shirley didn't just study. She also went out to work."

"Sorry, my studies and her work, that's what I meant."

"I understand your studies occupy a considerable part of your time."

"Almost my entire time."

"Were you faithful to Shirley?" I asked and saw that he was about to explode.

"You're not seriously asking me that!"

"I work in a job where I'm exposed to the weirdest stories you can imagine," I answered calmly.

"Then listen up! There was nothing odd or unusual between Shirley and me. Just a young couple starting along their way, who fate decided to separate under terrible circumstances. As I told you already, I loved Shirley. And even if we'd drifted apart a little during a stressful period, it didn't mean I didn't love her or was unfaithful to her. Who had time for cheating anyway?"

"Then, if I tell you that a co-worker of Shirley's is claiming that he had an affair with her, and that she intended to leave you for him, what would you say?"

He was silent, shocked.

"Yoni?" I asked after long minutes of silence. "Are you alright?"

"Does it look like I'm alright?" He grasped his forehead with both hands and started rocking back and forth in his seat. I had no doubt he had not known anything about the alleged affair between Shirley and Shai, unless, in addition to his medical studies, he was also taking acting classes.

"I'm really sorry you had to find out about it like this. To be honest, I thought you might have known. In a considerable number of cases, the partners know about an affair, or have guessed about it."

"Why should I suspect my fiancée? It wasn't like we'd been married for twenty years and were buried in routine. We were about to get married..." A large, round tear dripped from his eye. He rushed to wipe it away with the back of his hand. "I thought we were in love."

"I'm sorry."

"Who was he?" he asked in a trembling voice.

"Shai Hakim."

"Shai the Weirdo?"

"Yes."

His expression changed at once and he started laughing. "Then you can relax. There was no affair, just the fantasy of a delusional man. Shirley told me he had the hots for her."

"You sound very certain."

"I've no doubt about it."

"Why?"

"I told you, Shirley called him Shai the Weirdo. She realized he was infatuated with her, but she was kindhearted enough to feel sorry for him. Listen, even in a parallel universe, a guy like him and a girl like Shirley wouldn't become a couple."

"Why not? You said you hadn't met him."

"I could understand from Shirley's description that he

190

was a guy who didn't even come close to her level."

I could have told Yoni that Shai was an educated and sensitive guy, and could definitely fill the role of his deceased fiancée's partner, but I decided not to. All I wanted to do was to check if Yoni had known about the affair and if he had a motive. His reaction convinced me completely that he knew nothing. However, I could not, by any means, be convinced that the secret affair was only a figment of Shai's imagination.

Wednesday, June 29, 2011

I let the three new detainees spend the night in custody without knowing what they had been arrested for. I had not planned on letting them stew overnight, but Yoni's interview ended late, and I decided that a night of uncertainty might do what hours of interrogation could never do.

I decided to interrogate Lior first. My assumption was that he had acted as a messenger for Yaakov or Tom.

Lior was silent throughout the interrogation. I could not get out of him any single piece of information beyond a confirmation of his personal details. I presented him with the evidence: Nagusto's positive identification of him, and the lab's findings of his fingerprint, as well as Yaakov Sela's partial print, on the black washbag. Not a muscle on his face twitched, however. I remarked to myself that he would go far in the criminal career he had chosen for himself. Very few young and inexperienced felons succeeded in keeping silent like that.

After two hours of interrogation, I instructed the jailers to transfer him to an isolation cell and bring up Yaakov Sela.

Yaakov entered. He looked a lot less confident than he had two weeks ago. His body language projected distress and anxiety. I knew that, eight years previously, he had incriminated himself and had served time in order to protect his younger brother. Yaakov Sela acted like a tough and obstinate criminal toward strangers, but with his family, he conducted himself gently and with boundless love. It was his weak spot, and I was going to exploit it fully.

"Shalom, Yaakov. How are you?"

"Could be better," he responded and took a deep breath.

"I'm sure."

"Can you tell me why you arrested me, my son and my nephew?"

"Sure," I said and moved some of the papers lying on the desk closer to me, as if I had to refresh my memory about the facts. I knew them by heart. "Though I've a rather strong feeling that you definitely know why you're here."

"I've no idea."

"Two weeks ago, right in the middle of Tel-Aviv, two citizens were murdered: Koby Ozri - I know you knew him - and Shirley Navon, an accountancy student who was working near the site of the incident."

"You interrogated me already," he burst out angrily. "And I proved I wasn't connected to it at all."

"You proved nothing. The fact that, at the time we didn't find any evidence tying you to the incident, doesn't mean you weren't involved." I saw how the blood was flowing from his head to his feet. He understood that I had evidence against him. "In any case," I continued, "I'll start by telling you that the hired hitman has been caught. He confessed and identified Lior Zemach as the person who paid him for the assassination of Koby Ozri and Shirley Navon."

"Big deal," he tried to sound unflustered, without much success.

"Perhaps. Except that I have another piece of evidence. Believe it or not, the hitman you hired actually kept the washbag you used for the payment. The bag has Lior's fingerprints on it and also," I paused briefly for the dramatic effect, "your fingerprint."

He closed his eyes and grasped his head in his hands. If body language could constitute evidence of guilt, then Yaakov's entire body was one big confession.

"Yaakov, I want to be honest with you," I said, and he raised his eyes, looking defeated. "We've already interrogated Lior. He stuck to his right to keep silent. Listen, you can be proud of him as your protégé. I was very impressed by his ability to withstand the interrogation so well." Yaakov smiled a small, gloomy smile. "However, we both know that Lior is simply inexperienced and doesn't understand that, when the police have such strong evidence, keeping silent doesn't really help him. You also know that the person who interests me is the mastermind of the crime, not the messengers."

Yaakov's smile was erased. I could see that the wheels in his brain were spinning fast.

"In short, Yaakov," I tried to sum up, "I'm putting all my cards on the table. I know Lior was your messenger and that Nagusto, the hired hitman, committed the murder according to your instructions and planning. Nagusto has already signed an agreement with the District Attorney's office, and, I can promise you, there'll be no more agreements in this case. If you want to send your beloved nephew to prison for life because of an errand, then be my guest."

"It wasn't me who ordered this hit."

"The evidence shows otherwise."

"There are things you don't know."

"Like what? Like the fact that Shirley Navon's murder wasn't an accident?"

He stared at me, surprised.

"Well, don't be so shocked. I told you there's a witness agreement with Nagusto. He already clarified that point."

"It only proves I had no connection to this. What have I got to do with Shirley Navon?"

"I'm sure that if I dig long enough, I'll find the connection. But if you do me a favor and save me the effort, I promise you I'll throw in a good word to the D.A. on your behalf."

"You expect me to give you testimony in exchange for a good word?" He almost chuckled.

"I don't think you've any choice here. We both know I can submit the case to the D.A. as it is. If you want Lior to incur most of the charges, since this is what most of the evidence shows, no problem. I'm not saying it's the most robust case we've ever submitted, but we've put people in jail with a lot less. You know our rate of convictions very well."

"You said before you were interested in the dispatcher, not the messenger."

"Right."

"And suppose I was also a messenger?"

"Whose messenger?"

"I'm not talking without an agreement."

"Yaakov, nobody at the D.A. will approve another agreement in this case, and I don't have any reason to demand an agreement. The case against Lior is sufficiently strong. I believe you when you say you had no personal interest in Shirley Navon's death, which is why I want you to tell me what your motive was. The other option is for Lior to serve a life sentence instead of you. The D.A. won't ask for less than two consecutive life sentences, guaranteed. Let's be fair. You'll make my life easier, and I'll make your life easier. I give you my word."

"I believe you," Yaakov said after a brief silence. I was surprised. Even though I was quite certain that, in the end, he would consent and cooperate, I had thought this would take at least two days of discussions and consultations with his battery of lawyers. "You should know, Inspector Hadas, you have a good reputation. I know that if I reveal to you what I know, you'll meet me halfway."

I smiled and internalized the compliment. I was not a veteran at my job, but my word was trustworthy, always, and for everybody.

"I give you my word," I said solemnly.

"Then let's make an agreement between us. First of all, I'm asking you to release Tom. He has no connection to this thing. You can inspect and investigate, of course, but you said you were in the business of saving time."

"I'll look into it," I said, knowing that Tom would be released in the next twenty-four hours.

"Second, regarding Lior, my nephew, who's like a son to me. You said that the messenger didn't interest you, so I'm asking that you release him as well."

"There's evidence against him. It's impossible."

"He had no idea what it was about."

"That's not quite true. He didn't just deliver the bag. According to Nagusto, he also gave him instructions over the phone."

"They were all my instructions. He barely knew what it was about."

"I promise you we'll reduce his charges to the minimum possible, but it's not possible to exempt him totally. He knew he was sending a hitman to carry out a contract."

"He was only a messenger - my messenger - and I didn't initiate the murder, either. I didn't take out the contract. I received money for carrying it out."

"Then who took out the contract?"

"A girl named Sigal... not sure of her last name, but I have it written down somewhere. I know she worked with Shirley Navon."

CHAPTER 20

The Daffodils neighborhood of Ramat-Hasharon was renowned as one of the most sought-after neighborhoods in the Southern Sharon region. In fact, some would say it was one of the most sought-after and highly regarded neighborhoods in the entire State of Israel. It was a relatively new neighborhood, very close to the route to Tel-Aviv, and characterized by high-quality, well-spaced buildings, first-rate educational institutions, attractive streets and blooming gardens. The residents who populated the neighborhood - lawyers, CPAs and senior engineers - enjoyed a high socio-economic status. The price of the apartments in the neighborhood soared, and the residents enjoyed a pastoral tranquility in the center of the country.

It all changed in 2008.

Dorit Peleg-Sela, Yaakov Sela's eldest daughter, decided that she also wanted to enjoy that affluence, and moved into a magnificent penthouse apartment in the neighborhood. Her arrival shocked the residents. Many parents discretely checked the age of Dorit's children in order to ensure that their kids would not attend the same classes with them, and two families actually left the area. Rumor had it that the apartments of the families who left were sold at a loss. These rumors were very disturbing for most of the residents in the neighborhood; after years of steep appreciation, the value of their assets declined sharply, the way it happens wherever dubious individuals move into a neighborhood.

Dorit knew that people were talking about her behind her back. She was used to it. It was the price she had been paying all her life for being the daughter of one of the most notorious felons in the country. She, herself, did not interfere in the family business, not the legitimate ones, nor the others, but she had met her husband, Omer Peleg, because he had worked with her father. She took care not to interfere in his affairs, and whenever she was asked what her husband did, she answered, "He's a businessman."

In 2007, Omer was convicted and jailed for one year, but Dorit didn't even know what he had been charged with. When he had finished serving his time, she announced that they had to change their environment. She hired a realtor and asked him to find the best neighborhood in the area for her, and thus she arrived in the Daffodils neighborhood. In spite of the chilly reception she had encountered, Dorit believed that, like anywhere, she would find her place even in this prestigious neighborhood.

She was right. Even though it had taken several months, she succeeded in bonding with three girlfriends - Sharon and Rinat who were housewives like her, and Sigal, who worked in bookkeeping.

The four of them had moved to the neighborhood in order to attain a high standard of living and provide their kids with a high-quality education. However, they soon realized that they were pushed to the margins socially. They were too unsophisticated and not sufficiently educated, according to the standards of the other mothers.

They referred to themselves as the "Folksy Quartet," and enjoyed laughing at the rest of the residents of the neighborhood. They flaunted their wealth, dressed up in tight, fashionable clothes, and shared enviable pictures from their vacations and parties on social media, boasting with their well-shaped figures, which had not been degraded even though each of them had gone through at least three pregnancies. Their musical taste, which included Mizrahi singers like Eyal Golan, Koby Peretz and Shlomi Shabbat, was light years away from the accepted musical styles of the neighborhood. The four enjoyed reminiscing about the birthday parties they had organized for their kids, at which the other kids had been exposed to Mizrahi music for the first time. The little kids responded to the new sounds with joy and clapping, while their mothers rolled their eyes self-righteously. The Folksy Quartet knew that the other mothers regarded them as bad mothers - neglectful, even. But they reiterated to themselves that happy children had happy mothers, and enjoyed deriding the other mothers for being pretentious, reticent and sloppy.

Sharon, Rinat and Sigal preferred to ignore the heavy burden carried by Dorit's last name. They knew she was not involved in the family business, and focused on her attitude toward them. To them, she was the good-hearted, caring Dorit, who would do anything for her girlfriends. Sharon and Rinat, whose husbands were business partners and imported brand name products from China, knew that business was not entirely kosher in their families as well, and were not quick to judge others. Sigal was glad to have a warm, pleasant corner in the hostile neighborhood, where her senior position was not deemed prestigious enough since she had not studied at university.

When Sigal approached Dorit and told her that she needed her father's assistance, Dorit did not ask questions. She contacted her father and said that a good friend of hers needed his help. Yaakov asked for her phone number and promised his daughter that her friend would receive excellent service.

Yaakov contacted Sigal. She said she was at work and could not talk, and asked him to meet her in the evening, in the parking lot of the Industrial Park in Kfar-Saba.

Yaakov was not inclined to consent to such odd requests. However, since he had promised his daughter that he would help her friend, and since he was curious to find out what a bourgeois mother from Ramat Hasharon wanted from him, he agreed, and set up a late evening meeting with her.

Nothing had prepared him for what awaited him. Sigal was a good-looking, well-groomed woman. She slipped elegantly into his luxurious jeep, and Yaakov signaled his bodyguard to step outside.

"Thank you for agreeing to meet with me," she said, revealing a perfect smile.

"Any friend of Dorit is my friend."

"I'm glad to hear it, because what I'm about to ask you to do isn't something I'd ask just anybody."

"I can imagine."

"By the way, so that you don't misunderstand it, friends are friends, but I intend to pay you for the service I need. However, discretion is critical in this case."

"Obviously."

"I don't know what Dorit told you about me, but I work in a big communication company, in the Finance Department."

"She didn't tell me."

"I don't want to elaborate on this matter, but let's just say that I got in trouble. Serious trouble. I believe I can put my problem in order, but there's some girl who's on to me. That is, she doesn't really know it yet, but, in a few days, she'll figure out the entire business. She's already asking too many questions."

"So you want us to threaten her?"

"I don't want to live in fear," she said coldly. "I'd rather she simply didn't constitute a… sticky element."

Yaakov was stunned. "Then you simply want to eliminate her?"

"It seems to me that - yes, I do," she said without blinking. "Don't misunderstand me. I came to this decision with a heavy heart." Yaakov nodded, even though he found it hard to believe.

"This is a young woman without kids. I have four. If I go to jail, I'll sentence them to life without a mother. It's either me or her. And with all the pain and sorrow, especially when I think about my kids, then it's me."

Yaakov thought it over. Sigal had made a poor impression on him. He knew a few quite sordid criminals, but the woman sitting in his vehicle appeared to be worse than them. He could not sense one iota of morality or compassion in her. However, maybe it was only his feeling, and Sigal was behaving that way because she had found herself in a dead-end situation. Besides, Dorit had told him that Sigal was a good friend of hers, and he promised to help her. Yaakov loved keeping his promises.

Sigal told Yaakov that the best way to carry out the job without tracing it to her would be to make Shirley's death look like an unintended accident, an unfortunate victim in the battle between crime gangs.

"Then it was a double hit from the start?" I asked Yaakov when he had finished telling his story.

"No. I don't know what Nagusto told you, and you probably won't believe me. However, the instructions he received were to eliminate Shirley and injure Koby." I confirmed it by nodding. It was exactly what Nagusto had said. "Even though I knew Koby had been betraying us," he continued, "it was difficult for me to give an order that would lead to his death. We had many good years together. It hurt me to realize he was working with you. I wanted him to understand that he had to shut his mouth."

"And how did you coordinate it for Koby and Shirley to be in the same place?"

"Sigal informed me that Shirley used to go down to the Zelda Café and get takeout food from there two or three times a week. So one of my employees set up a meeting with Koby there. Nagusto was supposed to be on alert. In the event that Shirley did not go down there, we were going to postpone the whole thing for a day or two."

"But I understand that the entire operation was carried out at the first opportunity?"

"Right."

Alon was very satisfied with our progress, but claimed that the case was far from closed. What we had was the word of an organized crime chief against the word of a bookkeeper from Ramat Hasharon.

We could, of course, raid the Panda offices and carry out an audit of the financial system, where we expected to discover the large-scale embezzlement that had led to Shirley Navon's untimely death. However, we knew we might not find anything. It was possible that Sigal had already prepared herself for an interrogation and had managed to cover her tracks.

"In any case," said Alon, "at this stage, everything's circumstantial. Yaakov could have utilized his daughter's friendship with a Panda employee to cast the blame for the conspiracy on someone else."

I disagreed. All my instincts told me that Yaakov was telling the truth, but instincts were not sufficient evidence in Court.

I returned to the interrogation room and suggested that Yaakov meet with Sigal wearing a wire. Yaakov agreed. In order to disguise the meeting and make it look like a chance encounter, he suggested that they speak during the birthday party Dorit had organized for her son Ophir, who was his five-year-old grandson, on the roof of their home next Saturday.

Alon did not like the idea. He contended that releasing Yaakov was insane. After all, so much evidence connected him to the incident, including a confession. However, I insisted on it. I knew it could be a rare opportunity to catch Sigal red-handed, when she was least prepared. I told Alon that, in any case, Lior was still in detention, and Yaakov would not do anything to risk his beloved nephew.

Furthermore, I had no doubt that Yaakov would cooperate. I sensed that he did not really like Sigal, and definitely wished to entrap her. I hoped it would be the move that would tie up all the loose ends in the case.

CHAPTER 21

Saturday, July 2, 2011

The birthday party was planned for eleven. Yaakov asked Tom to drive there separately with his mother, saying he had to go to a brief meeting before the party. The brief meeting was with me and a technician. The technician attached a tiny microphone to Yaakov's chest and added a button-shaped camera to his shirt. We confirmed that the equipment was working properly and released him to go to the birthday party.

Yaakov's bodyguard was waiting at the entrance to the building where Dorit and Sigal's families lived. He was used to accompanying Yaakov everywhere, and had been a little surprised when asked to wait there, while Yaakov was somewhere else, alone. However, the bodyguard knew well enough to carry out his orders without asking questions. Yaakov assumed that the bodyguard was redundant, anyway, following his release from the detention center two days earlier. He was right. Two detectives were following him everywhere. During those two days, he had been one of the most protected citizens in the country.

I settled into the back seat of a police car disguised as a commercial vehicle, inserted some earphones, turned on the computer and watched Yaakov's live broadcast.

He and his bodyguard entered the elevator, joined by a young woman with a baby stroller and a young boy. The boy looked at the massive bodyguard with the menacing expression and clung to his mother.

"Are you going up to the birthday party?" asked Yaakov amiably.

"Yes," answered the woman, her voice trembling.

"Are you a friend of Ophir's?" Yaakov asked the petrified boy, his voice gentle. "I'm his grandfather."

The boy nodded. His mother stared at Yaakov and the bodyguard, terrified.

The elevator door opened and I saw Dorit. She was a very impressive woman, tall and statuesque. Contrary to what I had expected, her outfit was elegant rather than risqué. She wore a low-key dress, but it emphasized the curves of her body. She welcomed Yaakov with a warm hug.

"It's wonderful they released you in time for the birthday party," she whispered in his ear.

"Yes. Everything's alright," said Yaakov.

Dorit turned to look at the boy and said, "It's great to see you! Ophir asked when you were coming. You can go on up to the roof. A few kids are there already. Go ahead."

The boy ran off happily and disappeared inside the apartment.

"Oops, he forgot to take the gift," said the boy's mother, and produced a wrapped package from the baby stroller.

Dorit took the package from her and thanked her. "I'll tell Ophir it's from you," she added.

The woman turned around and returned to the elevator.

"The mothers don't stay for the party?" Yaakov asked nonchalantly.

"The kids are old enough to stay without their mothers."

"Really?" he chuckled. "They grow up so fast."

"Tell me about it…" said Dorit reflectively.

"Too bad… I wanted to meet Sigal, your friend," he said and my heart missed a beat. "You know, the one you asked me to help. I wanted to know if everything turned out alright."

"Sigal's not like the other mothers, she's family," Dorit smiled. "Of course she'll be at the party. She went with her family to visit her in-laws in Nahariya. They'll be here in a little while."

"Excellent," said Yaakov, and entered the apartment.

"Mother and Tom are already here," Dorit told him and closed the door. "Go on up."

Dorit went toward her designer kitchen and Yaakov turned toward an extravagant stairway near the entrance. The closer Yaakov got to the rooftop, the more noise I heard in the background. It was a mixture of kids shouting and music playing at an unreasonable volume. As soon as Yaakov set foot on the floor of the rooftop, a girl of about eight jumped on him and gave him a huge hug. I assumed it was another granddaughter of his. Ophir, the guest of honor, watched hypnotically as an adult dressed as a clown inflated a balloon, shaped it into a puppy, then handed it to him.

"Ophiri!" Yaakov called to the boy.

Ophir turned toward his grandfather and ran over to him, holding the balloon. "See what he made for me!" he said happily.

Yaakov lifted the boy into his arms and held him close in a warm hug. "What a beauty!" he said admiringly. "And what a great birthday party you're having!"

"All the kids think my birthday party's the best one ever!" the boy said proudly.

"It's because you're such a special boy and your parents love you so much." Yaakov kissed the boy warmly and lowered him back to the floor.

Omer, Ophir's father, approached Yaakov, shook his hand, and kissed him lightly on each cheek. "How are you?" he asked.

"Everything's fine," Yaakov said. "Where's Naomi?" he asked about his wife.

"I saw her near the buffet," he pointed to the other end of the roof, which was decorated with balloons and colorful ribbons. "She's busy setting up the food."

"What else?" chuckled Yaakov and went toward the buffet. On his way, he met Tom, who was sitting on a garden lounger with an older boy. They were engrossed in a game on the boy's cell phone.

"Hello there!" Yaakov tried to draw their attention. Tom looked up from the device, but the boy's eyes remained glued.

"Hi, Dad," said Tom. He got up and hugged his father. The youth didn't move. Tom kicked his leg lightly. "Say hello to your grandfather..." he said teasingly.

"Hi, Grandpa," said the boy unenthusiastically and lifted his head from the screen for a split second. Tom shook his head incredulously.

Yaakov said, "Drop it, let him finish his game. We'll talk later."

Tom sank back onto the lounger and was sucked into the game. I assumed there were a handful of people who dared to behave like that toward Yaakov Sela.

Yaakov continued toward the buffet. He stood quietly behind a woman who was arranging a stack of cupcakes and kissed the back of her neck. She jumped away with a start and the cakes dropped from her hands.

"Ay, Yaakov!" she said and put her hand on her chest.

"You scared me."

"Sorry," he said and laughed, amused by her reaction.

She hugged him and stroked his face gently. "Did you manage to do what you needed to?" she asked.

"Yes," he said, grabbing a cupcake from the stack.

She slapped his hand lightly. "Leave those for the kids!" she reprimanded him.

"It doesn't look like they'll miss it," he said, gesturing with his hand toward the buffet, which was loaded with cakes, cookies, snacks, fruits and candy.

"Dorit's really overdone it..." she chuckled.

"We know exactly who she got that from," he laughed.

She joined his laughter and took a cupcake for herself.

"Bon Appetit!" Dorit surprised them as they were enjoying the cakes. "Just don't forget to leave something for the kids," she said and placed two bottles of soft drink in the center of the table.

Yaakov and Naomi burst out laughing again.

"Where should I put these?" came a voice behind them.

Yaakov turned in the direction of the voice.

It was Sigal. She also held two bottles of soft drink in her hands.

"Put them there," Dorit said and gestured with her finger to the edge of the table.

"Sigal. How are you?" said Yaakov.

Sigal looked at him, puzzled. She smiled oddly and muttered that she was well.

"You two know each other?" asked Naomi, surprised.

"Yes, Sigal helped me with something to do with my income tax a few weeks ago."

"Don't you have your own CPA?"

"Don't worry, I'm not leaving Shimon, but I had a problem with something small. Sigal happened to know the supervisor at the Income Tax Authority, and he fixed the entire thing in two minutes."

"Good for you!" Naomi looked appreciatively at Sigal, who responded with an embarrassed smile.

The man in the magician's costume announced that he and Ophir were about to begin a spectacular magic show. The three women deserted the buffet and ran toward the improvised stage. Yaakov also turned in that direction and I had the opportunity to enjoy the magic show as well. Who said there were no perks in my line of work?

After a long session, the man announced an intermission and the kids thronged toward the lavish buffet. Yaakov used the opportunity, and finally approached Sigal.

"Did everything turn out as you wanted it in the end?" I heard him whisper to her, and I saw her chin moving up and down.

"Do you want to go talk somewhere quieter?" he whispered again. She nodded in a barely noticeable motion. "Where can I go for a little smoke?"

"Oh, Dad," Dorit grumbled. "Do you really have to?"

"Sweetie, you know I had a difficult week," he said in a slightly lower voice.

Dorit turned up her nose. "You can smoke on the living room balcony, but don't throw the cigarette butt down. The neighbors here really aren't nice."

I heard the sound of someone clearing her throat.

"Except for Sigal, of course," Dorit said, and smiled.

"Then I'll go down there for a few minutes. I have to make a few phone calls, anyway."

"Don't you dare miss the birthday cake," Dorit said menacingly and waved her finger.

"When is it?"

"In about twenty minutes."

"No problem."

Yaakov went down to the lower level, past the spacious, designer living room, and went out to the balcony overlooking a green park. I used the opportunity to call him.

"You're first-rate!" I complimented him.

"Thank you. I think I could have been a detective."

"It's possible," I laughed. "Listen, I assume Sigal will join you soon. It's important for me to remind you: I have to hear her say something that connects her to the story without a shadow of a doubt. Is it clear?"

"And what will happen then?"

"We'll make an immediate arrest."

"Really? In the middle of the birthday party? In front all of the kids?"

I thought quickly. "You're right. We'll wait until the party's over, but if Sigal leaves earlier, we'll have no choice."

"Actually, it looks like she'll stay till the end."

At that moment exactly, I heard the door to the balcony open. The monitor showed Sigal standing in the doorway.

"We'll talk later," Yaakov said and hung up.

"So, how are you?" he asked her.

"Nothing's simple," she said, coming closer.

"Don't worry, it'll work out."

"I heard you and Tom were arrested. Was it in relation to the murder at Zelda's?"

"Yes."

"Wow," she said in a worried voice. "That doesn't sound good."

"Don't worry. The police don't have a clue. They shoot in all directions, so they brought in a lot of people who had dealings with Koby Ozri. This is their line of inquiry. Nobody suspects that there's a connection to the girl."

"Yes, I know," she sighed. "I was also visited by an odd policewoman who started asking questions about Shirley, but it was something procedural."

"Don't worry," he said in a fatherly tone. "Nobody in the world would guess your connection to the story."

"I'm counting on you."

"I've got to say, your idea of eliminating her, supposedly by mistake, was a great idea. It'll steer the investigation away from you forever."

"Thank you," she said, and, to my amazement, she smiled briefly. "Before meeting with you, I read a story in the paper. It was an interview with a widower whose wife had been murdered - a case of mistaken identity. Her vehicle exploded when a bomb intended for an organized crime boss was planted in her car instead of his. It gave me the idea."

"Yes, I remember that case."

I remembered it, too. Tzila Yeruchami from Karmiel died in June 2008 because her vehicle was identical to the vehicle of one of the most notorious and dangerous criminals in Northern Israel.

"And how's everything now?" Yaakov continued.

"What do you mean?"

"Did it work out for you at the office?"

"I'm working on it. The main thing is that this Shirley's no longer sticking her nose in where it doesn't belong."

"I suggest you settle your problem as fast as possible, because if she was onto something, someone else may be, too. There's a limit to the number of accidental deaths that can happen in one department," he said lightly. She laughed.

"Don't worry. I'll have all my problems sorted out within six months at the most. Basically, most of the people in my company are lazy. Each one's doing only what he has to. The problem with Shirley was that she was far too keen." She wrinkled her nose.

"May I ask you something?"

"What?"

"Do you regret it?"

"Regret what?"

"What we did."

She thought for a moment and said, "I'm not glad that somebody died, but it was me or her, and I chose me. I know it may sound harsh, but I'm not a little girl. Life is harsh, and only the strong survive. I'm sure you agree with me."

"Sure."

"On a personal level, I don't miss her. I must admit, I couldn't stand her. But I wouldn't have thought of killing her like that if it hadn't been for her being so nosy."

I already had sufficient material to submit an indictment. I texted Yaakov, telling him that as far as I was concerned, I had what I needed. Yaakov moved on to discussing other things with her.

A few minutes later, Dorit yelled at them from above. "Are you coming to see Ophir blow out the candles?"

"Sure," they answered together and went up to the roof.

CHAPTER 22

The birthday party went on and on. After endless activities and surprises, the organizer announced that the party was over, extended his thanks to everybody and said cheerily, "See you next year!"

The parents arrived and took the young ones home one by one. When the last child had left, Sigal started picking up discarded wrappings and crushed candy from the floor.

"Leave it," Dorit scolded her.

"Look what a mess they left for you! You think I'd let you clean it up by yourself?"

"I'm not by myself," Dorit said. "My parents and brother are here, and the cleaner will be here tomorrow. I intend to tidy up a little and go rest, which is exactly what you should do. It's Saturday!"

Sigal smiled at Dorit and handed the garbage bag to Yaakov. She called her son and departed.

It was our signal to move in.

I summoned the two police cars waiting on the street nearby. I went up to Sigal's apartment with two plainclothes cops, while two other cops went up to Dorit's apartment to take Yaakov back to the detention center.

I knocked on the door and it opened right away. A weary-looking man stood in the doorway. He had the irritable look reserved for someone who had been disturbed during his Saturday siesta.

"Mr. Elad?" I asked briskly.

"Yes," he said impatiently.

"Is Sigal at home?"

His expression changed at once. He looked concerned.

"Yes. Has something happened?"

"Call her, please."

"Why? What happened? Who are you?"

"Israel Police," I said and flashed my ID. "I ask that you call Sigal here immediately."

"Alright, alright," he said, but by the time he turned around, Sigal was standing behind him.

"Rafi, who's disturbing us on a Saturday afternoon?" she asked, but fell quiet as soon as she saw me.

I nodded to one of the cops, and he went over to Sigal to handcuff her.

"Sigal Elad," I said formally, "in case you don't remember, my name is Hadas Levinger of the Israel Police. As of this moment, you are under arrest."

"Arrest?" Sigal's husband was shocked, Sigal a little less.

"I've a warrant for your arrest on suspicion of murder and conspiracy to commit a crime under aggravated circumstances."

"Murder?" The man repeated what I had said like an echo. "This must be a mistake!"

"No, sir, there's no mistake. I believe there are children in the house?"

"Right," he mumbled.

"Then I recommend you go and watch over them if you'd rather they didn't see their mother in handcuffs."

"Rafi, it must be a terrible mistake." Sigal finally opened

her mouth. "It's really best if you to go and watch the kids."

"I've no idea how you can be so calm, when -"

"I am not!" she said angrily. "Go!"

He turned around and went quickly to the children's room. I read Sigal her rights. I had a feeling she was going to stick to her right to remain silent until she saw a lawyer. However, before we reached the elevator, she asked to say goodbye to her children.

"Can you please take off the handcuffs?" she begged.

I agreed. One cop stood by the staircase, another remained by the elevator, and I accompanied her back to her apartment.

She went to the children's room, where Rafi and three of their children were sitting watching a cartoon.

"My sweeties," she said in choked voice, "Mommy has to go to an important meeting. I may not be able to come home today. Please be good for your dad."

"Alright," said the kids without looking up from the television screen.

Rafi stopped the movie. "Mommy's telling you that she may not come home today. Say goodbye to her nicely, and give her a hug and a kiss."

The kids got up with a noticeable lack of enthusiasm and went over to hug their mother. Sigal burst out crying.

"What's the matter?" asked the girl, who appeared to be the oldest of the three.

"Nothing," said Sigal and stroked her head gently. "I just remembered a sad movie I saw yesterday. When Lihi returns from Noa's, give her a big hug for me." She forced herself to smile and the kids returned to their movie.

"Shall we go?" I asked in a whisper and Sigal nodded.

As I expected, Sigal did not open her mouth. I tried to

talk to her, but she made it clear that she had no intention of saying anything before consulting a lawyer. I sent her to the detention center and drove home to salvage some of my own weekend.

Sunday, July 3, 2011

Sigal maintained her silence. She met with a lawyer and was instructed to adhere to her right to remain silent, to my regret. I was very eager to hear her version of the story. When I realized it was not going to happen at that stage, I thought I'd spend my time more usefully in a place that was completely unaware of the drama that had taken place in its hallways.

Equipped with a search warrant and a document disclosure warrant, I arrived at the Panda Company offices with a squad of investigators from the Economics Department of the police. I was welcomed again by Orna, the Human Resources V.P. When Orna saw the warrants and my entourage, she led us directly to the CEO's office.

The Panda CEO was sitting in a huge, extravagant boardroom. He was speaking to a handsome man, and they both looked worried. When we entered, they both stood up.

"Hello," said the executive, extending his hand to me. "Victor Frankel, CEO." He did not have to introduce himself. His picture and his name were frequently on the front pages.

I shook his hand. "It's nice to meet you. Inspector Hadas Levinger from the Israel Police," I said and was about to flash my police ID.

"It's alright," said Victor. "I believe you." I smiled and he

introduced the other man. "This is Yoel Porat, our
C.F.O.."

"Nice to meet you," I said and shook his hand.

I introduced the investigators by name and everybody
shook hands. "We're here to talk about something that's
been going on in your Finance Department," I said.
"Can we talk here?" Victor shook his head and turned to
Orna.

"Orna'leh, ask Natalee to open the large conference
room. There are too many people here to fit into my
office."

I looked around. The room was one of the biggest I had
ever seen. I supposed everyone had his own perception
of space.

Another girl entered the room, introduced herself as
Natalee, and asked us to follow her. We entered a
spacious conference room. Natalee asked what each of
us wanted to drink, went away, and returned after two or
three minutes with a tray loaded with refreshments. She
distributed the drinks efficiently, wished us a good day,
and closed the door behind her. Finally, we can get to
business, I thought.

"What about Guy?" Victor asked Orna the second the
door closed behind Natalee.

"He's on his way," answered Orna. "He's away this week,
at a CPA conference in Eilat. He's already there. I texted
him to get here urgently and he said he'd take the next
flight back. He'll be a while yet."

"It doesn't seem reasonable to wait for him," said Victor.
He turned to me. "Do you want to wait for Guy
Ditzman, our controller?"

"I think it's very important for him to be present, but
we're not going to wait here for several hours."

"You're right. You can start and we'll fill him in later."

I looked at the attentive expressions on Victor's, Orna's and Yoel's faces: three senior managers of one of the largest communications companies in the country. I knew I was about to make their world fall apart.

"I assume you haven't forgotten the tragic incident that occurred less than a month ago - the murder of Shirley Navon, your employee?"

"Of course not," they said almost in unison. "How could we forget something like that?" Orna added.

"I have very unpleasant news for you. Even though Shirley's murder was taken to be a regrettable accident, that was not, in fact, the case. I know this was how the media presented it, and the police didn't bother denying it. It was certainly our initial assumption that Shirley had been in the wrong place at the wrong time."

"You're not telling us that her murder was intentional?" said Yoel, his eyes wide open in shock.

"Regrettably, this is exactly what I'm saying. The assassination of Koby Ozri, the criminal who was also murdered in the same incident, was, in fact, just a cover, so that nobody would suspect Shirley was the real target."

"Why would anybody want to murder our Shirley?" asked Orna in choked voice. "She was such a lovely girl."

I took a deep breath and spat out the bomb. "Yesterday afternoon, we arrested Sigal Elad on suspicion of conspiracy to murder."

I saw the blood drain from the faces of Orna and Yoel. Victor looked at them apprehensively. "Can you remind me who she is?" he asked anxiously.

"Sigal works in the Controller's Department as a controller's assistant," said Orna.

"What exactly is she in charge of?" asked Victor.

"Payments to suppliers," answered Orna almost in a

whisper.

Victor's gaze froze. After a few moments, he turned to me and muttered, distressed, "Can you please explain to me what's going on here?"

"Certainly. After a strenuous investigation, there's credible suspicion that Mrs. Elad hired the services of a hitman to murder Shirley. The motive for the murder is not entirely clear, which is why we're here. It's our assumption that Mrs. Elad embezzled money from Panda, and that Shirley Navon discovered the embezzlement and died tragically as a result."

Orna started to sob. Yoel turned white and his mouth opened in shock. Victor moved his stunned gaze from one to the other.

"The purpose of my search warrant is to establish the motive. I'd like to go over your books with you. I believe we'll find something. If, in fact, we do find evidence of embezzlement, Panda can submit a criminal complaint against Mrs. Sigal Elad."

"Can we conduct the audit ourselves and deliver the findings to you?" asked Yoel.

"No. The audit's part of a police investigation, which is why any involvement of company employees or representatives is prohibited. We expect your cooperation, of course, but from this moment, all the Finance Department's employees are barred from accessing their workstations. Any such action will be deemed a criminal offense."

"You're not serious?" whispered Yoel.

"I'm very serious, regrettably. We don't want to allow potential for any accomplice to erase evidence during the audit."

"You think Sigal had an accomplice?" asked Orna, her voice distressed.

"We can't rule it out."

"No problem," Victor resumed his confident CEO tone. "You'll have our full assistance and support. Our objective is the same as yours."

"Definitely!" said Orna.

"I'm glad to hear that," I said. "Based on my experience in other cases, the most proper course of action is to notify all the department's employees that the system must be rebooted due to a technical problem, and to ask them to close all their files. Then, all the computer systems must be taken down in a systematic manner. That way, nobody can work concurrently with us, and no employee will have enough time to try to obstruct the evidence. When all the systems are taken down, the investigation will become active and we'll get down to business."

"How long do you think it will take?" Yoel asked with concern.

I looked in the direction of Gilad, the head of the investigation squad.

"It's hard for me to tell ahead of time," said Gilad. "It all depends on the complexity of the materials and the degree of cooperation we get from you."

"You'll have our full cooperation, you can be sure!" said Victor confidently.

"I'm glad to hear it, and I definitely believe it will shorten the investigation, but it's impossible to determine how long it'll take ahead of time. I can reassure you, since we have a suspect, and we already know roughly what we're looking for that, in most cases, we can allow the employees to return to work, at least partially, within twenty-four hours, depending on our findings."

"Excellent!" said Victor. "I'd like you to get started as soon as possible!"

About an hour later, the Finance Department of the Panda Company was almost deserted. Only the police investigators remained, along with two employees from the company's IT Department, who helped them get into Sigal's computer and other computers that were required for the audit.

At first, I tried to help the team, but soon realized that I was entirely redundant, and mainly a hindrance. Gilad and the other team members were CPAs or trained accountants, and they dived into the task with astonishing efficiency. I am not afraid of numbers or bank documents, but those inspections were definitely beyond my abilities. One of the investigators noticed my discomfort and asked if I was interested in checking the bookkeeping card index. It was clear, even to me, that the card index had no relevance to the audit, and that the suggestion had been designed to make me feel a little less useless. I took the fifty-page card index to a side office and started going over the numbers. Within five minutes, I was asleep.

Three hours later, the investigator who had given me the sleep-inducing materials entered the room.

"Hadas," he said in a whisper.

Twisted up from sleeping in an office chair, disheveled, and drooling slightly, I woke with a start. "What?" I shouted. "Ah, it's you!" I said, confused. "I've almost finished going over that index..."

"It's alright," he said in a relaxing tone. "It's not needed after all."

You don't say. "Great. It didn't look like there was anything there," I said in the most serious tone I could manage.

"Gilad wants to speak with you."

"Okay, I'll just hop over to the bathroom and then I'll

come straight up."

I ran to the bathroom and looked in the mirror. I looked terrible. I washed my face and tried to fix my hair to convey a less disheveled appearance. I didn't really succeed. I knew that anybody looking at me would instantly recognize that I had just woken up from a deep sleep. So be it.

Gilad was waiting for me in the conference room that I had been to the first time I came to the Panda Company. He looked fresh and alert. He radiated satisfaction. I knew that he was a brilliant CPA who had completed his internship in one of the leading firms in the country. He had received many job offers, but preferred to work for the police. We had a lot in common, except that, at that moment, he looked like someone who was about to crack a case, while I looked like someone who had dozed off during her watch.

"I dozed off a little," I confessed before sitting down across from him. "I've been working non-stop for over a week and -"

"It's alright," he laughed, "perfectly understandable. You don't have to apologize."

I smiled with embarrassment and sat down.

"I think I managed to crack Sigal's method, more or less. I can say with near-certainty that she didn't have any accomplices, certainly not within the company. As far as I'm concerned, if you approve, Panda can bring the accounting system for customers and sales back online, and allow the staff to resume their activities in full."

I peeked at my watch. It was six in the evening. Most of the employees would not return to work anyway, but there was no doubt in my mind that the news would make Victor and Yoel very happy.

"What about the rest of the systems?"

"I estimate within a day or two, everything can return to normal."

"That long? You said you'd cracked it -"

"I cracked the method, but not the extent of it."

"Ah… Well, explain to me what she did exactly?"

"Actually, nothing complicated, but, according to my experience, all the largest swindles are very simple in their basis. Sigal was actually paying the suppliers' invoices twice: once to the supplier, and again to herself."

"And how come they weren't on to her?"

"This was exactly the breach Sigal took advantage of. She made a transaction to the supplier, and then created a duplicate order against the transaction order she'd made before."

"A Storno order?"

"Yes, a cancellation order."

"But the Storno order didn't cancel the money transfer?"

"No. The Storno order only cancels the transaction in the company books, but it doesn't cancel the transfer itself. In reality, the supplier received the money, but in the books, the payment order was reopened. The repeat payment was transferred by Sigal to one of the fictitious accounts she'd opened for herself. At this stage, we've identified about five suspicious bank accounts."

"Interesting. Then, in fact, the supplier received the money twice, at least as far as the company was concerned – didn't he? So how didn't they notice it?"

"Very nice! Excellent point! Conducting a supplier's adjustment ought to be noticed. However, this company doesn't have any additional controls. And Sigal herself was in charge of the suppliers' adjustments! This is how she managed to conceal the whole thing."

"But how's it possible to hide such embezzlement?"

"This is a question for the bookkeepers. Sigal knew very well where to take the money from. She was sufficiently smart not to repeat the trick with the same supplier too many times, and she transferred the money she withdrew to all kinds of budgetary pits that could swallow such sums. According to what I've seen so far, she never withdrew very large sums at one time, only up to 50,000 Shekels, no more. I know that for me and you, it's a lot of money, but for Panda, it's pocket money."

"I still don't understand how nobody figured it out. After all, there are managers here, there are accountants.... Sorry, I still don't see how she was getting away with it."

"Shirley Navon probably figured it out. That's why we're here," Gilad reminded me and winked. No doubt he was very satisfied.

"Clearly. The question is why nobody else noticed that money was missing..."

"It can happen in such a big company. I'm not surprised the public accountants didn't detect the deception. I can't tell you yet how much money she stole exactly, but it runs to millions."

"Millions?" I was shocked.

"Yes, millions. It didn't happen in one day, but over a long period. She didn't steal one large sum, but rather many relatively small sums. There's a term for this in the auditing field. It's called 'the threshold of substantiality.'"

"What does it mean?"

"In every company, there's an audit team that sets up a certain threshold. Sums under that threshold aren't checked because there's no benefit or interest in checking them. I'd bet that the threshold of substantiality at Panda was at least a 100,000 Shekels. Sigal knew very well what the threshold of substantiality was, and took care never to exceed it."

"So - even if, by chance, someone were to suspect that something odd was going on - it wouldn't have been checked because it concerned insubstantial sums."

"Exactly!" Gilad smiled. "We have here a quite sophisticated woman who was very familiar with the auditing policies and procedures, and knew how to fool the CPAs."

"As far as I remember from my previous investigation here, she wasn't a CPA herself."

"That makes sense. Many public accountants aren't really familiar with the work bookkeepers do, and don't understand it."

"You're not the first to tell me that," I said and made an effort to remember where I had heard this sentence before.

"Usually, bookkeepers are the ones saying it, but aren't taken seriously. However, I've interrogated so many bookkeepers who managed to fool public accountants that I know this is the sad truth."

"I remember who told me that! Shai Hakim, who works here."

"What's his position?"

"Bookkeeper." I smiled. Gilad responded with a big grin.

CHAPTER 23

Monday, July 4, 2011

Gilad and his team worked in the Panda offices until the small hours. In the morning, he called me and told me that it was time to bring the company directors together to review the extent of the embezzlement. I asked him if he still thought that nobody from the company had collaborated with Sigal, and he answered affirmatively. I told him to get some sleep and summoned Rafi Elad, Sigal's husband, for interrogation.

Rafi entered the station frightened and confused. I greeted him and led him to the interrogation room. He needed several long minutes and two glasses of water to calm down the tremors that had overtaken his body.

"Can we begin?" I asked.

"Y-yes," he said in a broken voice. "I apologize for being like this. I'm just very agitated and I don't understand what's going on."

Either he was an excellent actor, or he had been living in a fantasy world, with the lights just turned on in the auditorium, I thought to myself.

"Is your name Rafael Elad?"

"Rafi's fine."

"Okay. Rafi, as you know, your wife has been detained on suspicion of conspiracy to commit murder in aggravated circumstances."

"I'm still in shock -"

"Why?"

"I find it hard to believe."

"Really?" I asked in a skeptical tone.

"Yes, really!" He almost shouted. "I've been married to this woman for fifteen years, and we have four children! You don't think I'd be shocked? She's been arrested for murder!"

"Do you believe your wife's innocent?"

"I definitely want to believe it."

"Tell me a little about yourself. What do you do?"

"I'm a sales rep for the Strauss Group."

"So you travel around to supermarkets and grocery stores and market the merchandise."

"Something like that."

"How much do you make in a month?"

"Em…" He was stammering again. "I don't know exactly. Are you asking gross or net? I have all kinds of sales rep commissions -"

"What's your average net income, more or less?"

"I think it's 10,000 Shekels a month, more or less."

"Not bad," I smiled. "If there's an opening for a sales rep, let me know." He failed to smile at my weak joke. "Do you have any idea of Sigal's net income?"

"Actually, no. She takes care of our finances. She's a bookkeeper, as you know."

"If I told you that her net monthly salary is 8000 Shekels, would that sound about right?"

"Yes."

"Do you have a mortgage on your apartment?"

"No, to the best of my knowledge."

"You have a Honda Accord 2010, and you've travelled abroad seven times over the last two years."

"We didn't always travel together. Mostly, she traveled with her girlfriends."

"Okay. What I'd like to ask you is this: where does the money come from?"

"Money for what?"

"For an apartment in a prestigious neighborhood, for a new car, for traveling abroad. Together, the two of you make 18,000 Shekels per month. It's very nice, but I don't have to be a mathematical genius to realize that it's really not enough to manage a household like yours."

"I'm not really involved in these matters. Sigal deals with all the bills. However, a few years ago we received a very large sum of money, Sigal's inheritance from her uncle."

"What uncle? What's his name?"

"I didn't know him. Sigal didn't really know him, either."

"What was the amount of the inheritance?"

"Not small. Several million."

"Wow! Not a small amount from an uncle you didn't even know!"

"Yes. I was surprised, too, but I was simply happy we could afford the apartment in Ramat Hasharon."

"Do you remember when, more or less, that rich uncle had died and left you the money?"

"Five or six years ago."

"Do you have an idea how much money you received, and where it was deposited?"

"Not really. I told you, it was all Sigal's responsibility. I understood from her that we didn't receive all the money at once. There were all kinds of assets that had to be sold, so we received the money in installments."

"I see. Did Sigal appear to be under pressure lately?"

"In what sense?"

"Was she concerned about work?"

"No more than usual."

"Was she relaxed in general?"

"No," he said, and lowered his eyes. "Sigal's not a relaxed sort of person, for better or worse. That's why I'm with her. They say opposites attract. She's fire and I'm water."

"Can you explain?"

"She always says she's raising five children," he chuckled bitterly. "She managed the household from the moment we got married. In fact, from the moment we met."

"Is she a strong woman?"

"Very."

"Rafi, I'm sorry to tell you that, in addition to conspiracy to commit murder, there's an additional suspicion associated with your wife."

"What?"

"The motive for the murder. According to an investigation being conducted right now at Panda, it looks like Sigal embezzled money from the company. I assume the story about the uncle never happened and he never even existed."

"It can't be! She showed me documents!"

"Do you have them?"

"They're probably at home somewhere."

"Did you ever have any idea that a considerable portion of your money actually originated from Panda?"

"No!" he said, and it was apparent that the question hurt him. "I told you, to the best of my knowledge, we had money from an inheritance."

"We'll examine this avenue in more detail," I told him, even though it was clear to me that we would not find any mysterious rich uncle.

I left the room and requested that Sigal be brought over

for interrogation. I instructed the cop to take Rafi out of the room precisely as Sigal was approaching along the hallway.

"Rafi!" Sigal shouted in a choked voice. "What are you doing here? Who's with the kids?"

"My mother's with them," he answered with agitation and asked the cop if he could go over and hug his wife. The cop naturally prohibited him from approaching her. Sigal burst into tears.

"But what are you doing here?" she asked tearfully.

She did not receive an answer. The policewoman escorting her broke off their conversation and pulled her along to the interrogation room. "Why can't I speak with him for a moment?" Sigal sobbed.

"There are visiting hours for that," answered the policewoman coldly, and brought Sigal into the interrogation room. I entered the room and the policewoman left. Sigal was crying bitterly. I took out a box of tissues from the locker in the corner and handed it to her. She pulled out a tissue and wiped her nose.

"Has something happened?" I asked.

"Nothing," she said, regaining her self-control in an amazing speed. "I'm sure you understand this isn't easy for me."

"No doubt," I said and sat down opposite her. "Sigal, the reason I brought you here today is to inform you that we have evidence concerning the money you stole from the Panda Company."

She looked at me with a frozen expression. Even seasoned criminals had expressed more emotion than this when I hurled accusations at them. "I must admit, your silence up to this point has been rather impressive. If you want to keep quiet, or consult again with your lawyer, you can. However, the evidence against you is sufficiently strong for us to gain a conviction without an admission of guilt on your part. You have to understand that, at this point, there are two criminal cases against you. In one, you're charged with conspiracy to commit murder, in the other you're charged with theft. My problem in your case is that I find it hard to believe or comprehend how you did it all by yourself." I stopped for a moment and fixed my eyes on her piercingly. "I noticed you saw Rafi here a few minutes earlier. You probably want to know why he's here. Let me explain. I brought him in for interrogation because I suspect that he's your accomplice. I couldn't understand how a family with a combined monthly salary below 20,000 Shekels could afford a standard of living appropriate to people who earn three or four times that - without both spouses being well aware of the source of the income."

Tears were pouring from Sigal's eyes once more. She did not say a thing, but I knew that she was deducing the simple conclusion by herself. If she continued to keep quiet and did not cooperate, she would get her husband mixed up in it and arrested as well, and their kids would be taken into care.

"Rafi claims he didn't know anything," I decided to help her. "He has a preposterous story about a mysterious, rich uncle who bequeathed millions to you."

Sigal closed her eyes and then said, "It's not a story!"

"There actually was a rich uncle?" I asked and kept myself from laughing.

"No. But this is what Rafi thinks. I beg you, leave him alone. He doesn't know anything."

"Doesn't know about what?"

She closed her eyes again, swallowed and said quietly, "He doesn't know what I was doing."

"And what did you do, Sigal?"

"Everything you say... I did it all," she said and resumed crying.

I waited a few minutes until her sobbing subsided.

"Can you tell me what happened, in your own words?" I asked gently.

Sigal Elad was the sixth child in a low-income family. Her parents were busy day and night providing for the family, and her older siblings were busy with their own affairs. Sigal raised herself and learned to stand her ground from an early age. She was a bright pupil, especially in math, but received low grades due to undiagnosed learning disabilities. Years later, she identified the same difficulties in her eldest daughter, but, fortunately, she could provide her with the right tools to achieve proper grades. When she grew up, she had to attend a vocational high school because her grades were too low for a regular high school. She decided to study clerical work and bookkeeping, and received a bookkeeper's diploma. Due to her family's strained financial situation, she was exempt from military service. Upon completing her studies, she started working for a clothing importer in South Tel-Aviv. She picked up the skills very fast and realized that she liked the field. She wanted to study for a degree in Accountancy, but since she had not matriculated from a regular high school, the gates of the university were closed to her. In view of that, she supplemented her education with professional courses and advanced slowly to more significant positions.

When she was working for a public accounting firm, she had to deal with interns who did not understand numbers as well as she did, but had enjoyed better luck in life. She knew that, if she only had the opportunity to study at university, she could have been an outstanding student. However, the years passed, she met Rafi, married him, had children, and her dreams vanished little by little.

Working for Panda was rather convenient. When Sigal first started there, the Israeli cellular market had been in its infancy. She saw before her eyes how the company as a whole, and the Finance Department in particular, were growing. She was shocked to realize, time after time, how scanty the knowledge of the university graduates was, and how superficial their understanding of the accounting system. She was deeply disappointed when they were placed higher in the organizational hierarchy and on a higher salary grade. When the company went public, the senior employees received options and stocks. Due to her lower rank, Sigal only received options worth less than half her monthly salary.

The insult had been hard to bear. Sigal was deeply hurt. After all, she had been one of the most loyal employees, and had contributed so much to the company's growth. Why wasn't she granted the proper recognition?

She approached her supervisors and pointed it out to them. In return, she received a separate office the size of a closet and the title "controller's assistant," which was worthless in terms of salary.

Her first theft was unplanned. Sigal accidentally deleted a payment order, and consequently discovered the fault in the system. When it happened, Sigal was already disposed to committing the embezzlement, so she exploited the opportunity she had run into. She calculated how many shares she would have received, and what their value would have been, and decided that this would be the sum she would transfer for herself. She told herself that she was entitled to that money by right, so there was no reason not to take it.

Within two years, she had transferred to herself all the money she planned was hers by right. However, the new standard of living she had grown accustomed to became addictive. She continued to transfer money, perfecting her methods as she went. She told her husband that the money was an inheritance from a mysterious rich uncle, and showed him forged documents as evidence.

She also told her co-workers that the rise in her standard of living had been due to an inheritance, except that she told them that it was from her husband's uncle. Nobody suspected anything. Many at Panda even admired her for continuing working in spite of her new-found wealth, even though she had asked to cut down her work hours in order to spend more time with her kids.

Sigal knew that she should stop the money transfers. She felt worse with each transfer, but found a justification for each of them - her daughter's Bat-Mitzvah party, assisting her ailing father, a wedding gift for her beloved nephew, and more. She decided to take a course on the capital market and invest a part of the transferred money in various funds, so that she could return the money she had stolen and keep her high standard of living at the same time. She had self-confidence, excellent analytical skills, and she counted on her continuing success. However, the global economic crisis of 2008 shattered her plans. Investing in the capital market became too risky.

When Shirley Navon started working for Panda, Sigal did not even notice her existence. When it was decided that Shirley would stay with the company, she was teamed up with Sigal to help her with everything related to supplier payments. At first, Sigal thought that Shirley was like all the other Economics and Accountancy students: snobs so busy calculating their way to the top that they would rather not spend time on their dull, routine work. Soon, she found out that Shirley was made of an entirely different substance. It was hard not to like her. Apart from her attractive, pleasing appearance, Shirley had been endowed with a radiant personality. She was always eager to help, never flinched from doing the dirty work, and was the only one who behaved affably toward Shai Hakim, the department weirdo.

The whole story had actually started during the Passover vacation, almost two months before the murder. Most of Panda's employees were on vacation. Sigal made sure that her vacations were not too long and that they overlapped the general vacations, so that nobody would meddle with her computer. She did not realize that Shirley had asked to work during Passover to earn some overtime. On one of those days, a supplier called the department to find out why his payment had been delayed. Shirley checked his card and noticed a cancellation order for the sum of 58,000 Shekels. She asked the supplier if he had received that sum, and he said he had, indeed, received it, and that he wanted to check about another sum. Shirley's suspicion was sparked.

When Sigal returned from her vacation, Shirley asked her about it. Sigal explained that, orders were sometimes corrected because of changes to a bank account or something like that, and that everything was alright.

Sigal thought that this was the end of the story. However, Shirley ran into a similar order a few days later, and again asked Sigal about it. Sigal provided some sort of excuse, but noticed an odd flicker in Shirley's eyes. It appeared to her that Shirley did not believe her. That day, Sigal stayed after hours. When Shirley finished work and the floor was deserted, Sigal went over to the workstations in the open space. Shirley's workstation was well-organized, and Sigal did not find anything suspicious there. However, Sigal did not want to take any chances. She turned on the computer and entered the standard password each employee received upon joining the company. To her delight, Shirley had not changed her password. Sigal opened Shirley's mailbox. Among the incoming messages was a message from the Service Department of the software house. Sigal was devastated. Shirley had sent a query about Storno money movements.

There was no room for doubt. Shirley was suspicious. Sigal realized that, when Shirley delved deeper, she would discover the truth. Sigal deleted the response message from the software house and decided to load Shirley with plenty of work so that she would forget about it.

That was on Thursday. By Sunday, Sigal had changed her mind. She realized that a heavy workload could only be a temporary, partial solution, and that the only way to prevent Shirley from getting to her was to eliminate her.

"Didn't you have any feelings of guilt?" I asked her.

"I had, and still have, lots of feelings of guilt," she said without sounding too sincere. "It's hard for me to explain my feelings during that period. I was stressed out. I had my back to the wall. I didn't want to be separated from my kids."

"Do you now realize that you'll be separated from them for many years?"

"Yes," she said and started crying again.

CHAPTER 24

Panda's conference room was set up for one of the most difficult meetings in the company's history. I arrived with Gilad about fifteen minutes before the scheduled time of the meeting. We sat down in the same seats we had used last time we were in this room, but then we noticed name tags at each place, indicating a formal seating plan. We searched for our names and were surprised to see that we had been placed to the right of the CEO. I studied the name tags. In addition to Orna, Guy and Yoel, whom I had already met, I saw the names of several managers, members of the board of directors and representatives from the public accounting firm representing the company.

Two grim-looking young women placed bottles of soft drinks on the conference table and asked us if we would prefer hot drinks. Gilad asked for a long espresso and his request was promptly fulfilled.

Within a few minutes, the room was full of men in suits. Gilad and I stood out in our jeans and tricot shirts. There was a rumble of whispers and agitated murmurs in the air, which stopped the minute Victor Frankel entered the room.

Victor went slowly to his seat, looked at me and said

dramatically, "Dear friends, we have convened here today for an emergency meeting due to an extremely irregular incident that took place in our organization. I thank all of you for coming at such short notice. I know that, for some of you, it was a genuine inconvenience. Even though I can guess that most of you know more or less what's involved, I'd like to dissolve the vague rumors and explain the difficult situation in which we're caught up."

He paused, took a deep breath and continued. "We have two police investigators with us," he pointed to his right, "who will give you the details of their findings later, but I'll provide you with the background. Less than a month ago, we lost a young promising employee, Shirley Navon. Shirley was a bright Accountancy student who worked in our Finance Department. Her death was presumed to be a regrettable accident in the crossfire between crime gangs. However, the police investigation revealed that the hit was directed at Shirley herself."

Cries of astonishment were heard around the conference room. Victor asked to continue and the voices subsided. "The investigation suggests that the one who initiated this heinous murder is, in all likelihood, another Panda employee, a veteran and esteemed employee in the Finance Department - Mrs. Sigal Elad."

This time it was difficult to quell the cries of astonishment. Victor was compelled to knock on the desk in order to silence them. "To the best of my understanding," he continued when the room was silent again, "Mrs. Elad has refused to admit any culpability. However, the evidence collected has determined that her motive was embezzlement of company money, which Shirley Navon had discovered by chance."

The rumblings were building again. Victor allowed his

employees to digest his words and waited until the room was silent again.

"I'll let these capable, talented police investigators who cracked the case swiftly and efficiently, have the floor now," Victor concluded, and he sat down.

I got up and looked at the attendees. Their expressions indicated that the situation was unfamiliar for them.

"Shalom. I'm inspector Hadas Levinger, in charge of the murder investigation of the late Shirley Navon and Koby Ozri. Mr. Frankel related the chain of events very well and there's no need for me to expand upon it, except to give you a minor update. A little earlier, the suspect admitted her involvement in conspiracy to commit murder and in embezzling money from Panda in the course of her work as a controller's assistant."

I took a deep breath and allowed my words to sink in. Any hopes some people may have had that it was all a regrettable mistake faded away. "Before we convened here, I met with my colleague, Gilad Shavit. Gilad is a public accountant and financial investigator for the Israel Police. According to the data, over the last five years, Sigal stole at least ten million Shekels."

A ruckus broke out in the room. Yoel and the public accounting firm's representatives started to exchange vigorous whispers and passed folders and documents between them. Victor Frankel held his head in his hands and turned to Orna, who was sitting to his left, and showered her with questions.

Gilad had made it clear to me ahead of the meeting that, although it was a large and significant sum that would cause upheaval at Panda, it would not shatter the company. The Panda Company's business cycle stood at approximately two billion Shekels per year. During the last five years, when the embezzlement had taken place, the net profit had not dropped below seventy million US Dollars per year. The sum of ten million Shekels was not substantial for a company the size of Panda, but the damage to its image, once the story went public, would be enormous.

When the ruckus subsided, I invited Gilad to explain the manner in which the embezzlement had been carried out.

Gilad thanked me and started detailing Sigal's methods, and how she had used the tools of the system to transfer money to her own accounts. The explanation was rather simple, but some of those present had difficulty understanding it and asked many questions. To cut short an exhausting series of repeated questions, a member of the board of directors, who had been silent up to that moment, writing comments for himself in a small notebook, stood up and asked to speak.

"If I understand correctly," he said, and looked at his notebook, "for at least five years, a lower ranking employee was actually conducting duplicate expense registration. The first time, she paid the supplier who had, indeed, provided the service, and the second time the expense was registered against a payment made to her personal account."

"You understood perfectly," Gilad smiled. It appeared that the penny finally dropped after an hour of explanation.

"What I don't understand," the man continued and turned to look at the public accounting firm's representatives and the C.F.O., "is this: how could it happen that, for five years, duplicate expenses were registered, money was transferred to accounts that did not belong to the suppliers, and nobody noticed? Don't we have any internal controls? Where were the public accountants for five years? This embezzlement involves fictitious expenses in the order of millions. How come nobody noticed?"

"Ephraim," said Victor, "I don't think this is the time or the place."

"Why not?" Ephraim burst out. "This is *exactly* the time and the place. I'm tired of being silenced in board meetings. How many times do I have to say that the Finance Department is managed unprofessionally and that the public accountants do not conduct a sufficiently good audit?"

"Do me a favor," called out Yoel. "You have your own agenda. You want a different C.F.O. instead of me - you want your friend as the company CPA!"

"Enough!" Victor got up and pounded the desk with the palm of his hand. The pounding was so strong that I was afraid the desk would fall apart. I looked at Victor's palm. It was red. Victor clasped it with his other hand to alleviate the pain. "We're in a very sensitive situation. It's unnecessary to add fuel to the fire." Orna nodded in agreement. There were tears in her eyes.

Victor sat down and continued massaging his sore hand. "Shlomo," he turned to the public accounting firm's representative. "I also would be happy to understand how, indeed, you failed to detect this embezzlement during your audits."

Shlomo smoothed his tie with his hand, cleared his throat, smiled a little smile and delivered a short, formal speech that, I had no doubt, he had prepared in advance.

"Victor, management, and board members - I regret that we have to attend such a difficult meeting. However, I cannot respond to financial questions without seeing the complete data. I would be obliged if the esteemed investigators could transfer the relevant materials to me so that we can study them and respond to them."

He turned to look at me and stretched his lips in a thin smile. I responded with a wide smile.

"I certainly don't underestimate the police investigation," he continued. "And I believe there is something to it. However, as is well known, my profession is not one of belief, but one of knowledge. Therefore, everything I will say now is based on the assumption that the investigation's results are, indeed, correct, and embezzlement actually took place in the company. It's very important for me to clarify a few points: the audits we conduct within the company are only samples. We do not go over, nor are we supposed to go over, *all* the company's records. In addition, it is not our job to look for and find embezzlement. If we find evidence of embezzlement during our routine audits, it is our duty to report it. I emphasize, we do not have a legal or ethical obligation to detect embezzlement."

"So you mean to tell me," Victor cut him off, "that were it not for Shirley Navon's alertness, Sigal would have continued to steal from the company quietly for many more years?"

"That's not what I said. Any embezzlement is exposed in the end," said Shlomo. "It's only a matter of time. According to the description given to us by the investigator earlier, I can say that embezzlement on such a scale points to a problem in the company's policies and procedures, and its internal controls. I've no doubt there's a loophole that made this embezzlement possible. Our office, by the way, has an internal controls department, and it can provide comprehensive internal control review and identify additional problems and lapses."

"For an additional fee, I'm sure!" Ephraim could not

restrain himself again.

Victor's eyes seemed ready to shoot arrows of fire at the insubordinate board member, but this time the veteran public accountant retorted. "Yes, Ephraim, for an additional fee." He emphasized the last two words and continued. "We are professionals, and there's no reason not to be compensated for our difficult, professional work. You don't sit here on a voluntary basis, either." Ephraim lowered his eyes like a scolded kid.

The meeting was adjourned and people started to disperse. Victor asked Gilad and me to stay in the room.

"I'd like to thank both of you," he said after the last attendee had left and his assistant, Natalee, had closed the door. "You did an exceptional job. If you ever decide to leave the police, I'd like to be the first to know about it."

"Thank you," we both said in unison, and giggled in embarrassment.

"I'm sorry you had to witness our dirty laundry, but I'm sure you're used to it."

"We've seen dirtier laundry," laughed Gilad.

"Gilad, you're a CPA, right?"

"True."

"I'd like to ask you about the discussion that took place here. Was the public accountant right? Is he really not supposed to detect such embezzlement?"

"I agree with him on principle. It's not the job of the public accountant to search for embezzlement. He's not required to check all the records, but, like he said, to conduct a sample audit. I also agree with his assumption that it's difficult to identify fraud on such a scale. It involved a small sum, relatively, for Panda."

"Then, in your opinion, it wasn't possible to detect the embezzlement?"

"I'm not sure of that at all. I agree with Shlomo that, at some stage, the fraud would have been discovered, but probably from within the organization and not through his audit. The fact is, the person who detected the problem - and because of it, she's no longer with us - was a Panda employee, not someone from the public accounting firm. Personally, I think there's a blunder in the study of Accountancy, and therefore the chance that a public accounting firm will detect such fraud is close to zero. Don't think for a moment that another firm would have done a better job. Those who actually conduct the audits are interns or rookie public accountants. They don't have the tools or the knowledge to examine the data thoroughly. Regrettably, this case won't change the regulations. It concerns a small embezzlement. The one to incur the consequences will be only the defendant. When there are more substantial embezzlements, like the affair that led to the Enron crash in the United States a decade ago, or the embezzlement of Ettie Alon, which crushed the Israel Commerce Bank, then the legislature intervenes and procedures get changed."

Victor was listening, his forehead wrinkled.

"If you want," Gilad said in an attempt to reassure him, "I can recommend a few consultants in the field who can conduct a review of your internal controls and provide recommendations for new policies and procedures."

"That sounds exactly what we need. Thank you," said Victor.

We went down together to the lobby. The concourse in front of the building was bustling with journalists and news crews.

Victor explained the chain of events concisely. Then we answered a few questions. It was evening. I knew what the news broadcasts would open with tonight.

"I'm beat," I told Gilad when the improvised press conference was concluded.

"Do you want to get something to eat?"

"That would be nice," I said. "There are several nice cafés around here."

We walked several yards and stopped in front of the Zelda Café. The shuttered display window had been replaced with a new window that was still marked with wide duct tape.

"You want to eat here?" asked Gilad.

I nodded and we stepped inside.

DEAR READERS

In the last chapter of the book you have just read, it was proposed that it was not the job of the public accountant to detect embezzlement.

Before I get into the depth of the matter, I'd like to diffuse the vagueness concerning anything associated with the profession of Accountancy, which, regrettably, a considerable part of the population does not understand – not its purpose, nor its function.

Accountancy is a field that deals with the recording of financial data. The majority of financial recording existing today is based on bookkeeping, which is a method of recording financial transactions. The most common bookkeeping method in the world is the double entry method, which was developed at the end of the fifteenth century by an Italian friar named Luca Pacioli.

Public Accounting, in contrast, is a more recent profession that developed in the nineteenth century, during the Industrial Revolution. The background for the development of the profession was the dissociation of capital owners from managing businesses and the establishment of corporations. The capital owners received financial reports from the company managers, and wanted to know if the reports reflected the company's condition accurately. Thus, the need for an external agent to examine the reports was created, and a new profession was born: the public accountant.

A public accountant is a reviewer. He arrives at the company, reviews the financial records and the financial reports, and confirms that they do not contain substantial errors. Due to the nature of his work, a public accountant cannot be a company employee, but rather an external agent.

The first page of any financial report, after the cover page and the table of contents, is the public accountant's letter directed to the stockholders. The letter's wording is usually fixed, unless the report includes unusual findings. I offer here a section from the fixed version; the emphasis is mine.

"We conducted our audit according to the auditing standards acceptable in Israel, including the standards set in the Public Accountants Regulations (the Public Accountant's Way of Conduct) of 5733 – 1973. According to these standards, we are required to plan the audit and conduct it for the purpose of achieving a **reasonable measure** of certainty that the financial reports do not constitute a substantially erroneous presentation.

An audit includes a **sample check** of evidence that support the amounts and the information in the financial reports. An audit also includes a review of the accounting principles that were implemented and of the substantial estimates **made by the company's management and board of directors,** as well as an estimate of the suitability of the financial reports' presentation in its entirety. We think that our audit and our other public accountants' reports provide an appropriate basis for our expert opinion."

This is the Israeli version, which is not substantially different from the acceptable wording in many countries around the world. Many capital owners tend to skip this letter and go directly to the financial report itself, i.e., to the profit and loss report and the rest of the reports and the analyses. However, the letter is an important document, which, in fact, clarifies the nature of the public accountant's job. I emphasized words which clarify two important points:

1. The audit is conducted based on a sample.
2. The report is, in fact, a report by the company management, and the public accountant only expresses his opinion on the report.

So much for the theory. Let's move on to reality.

I will describe reality through my personal story and the road I traveled in the profession I chose for myself. I completed my Accountancy studies at Tel-Aviv University in 1999, and started working right away as an intern in a public accounting firm that had been the Israeli representative of one of the largest public accounting firms in the world.

At the end of 2001, one of the world's gigantic energy companies collapsed. The reason for the collapse was a deliberately erroneous accounting report. The firm where I worked was the one representing the American energy company.

At that time, I was completing my internship. The saga of the collapse of the energy company affected me personally. The firm for which I worked gradually crumbled, and is, today, part of another firm. Like many others, I looked for a new job. I decided to leave the field of public accounting and auditing and crossed over to the other side – the side of private accounting and bookkeeping.

I started working for a relatively small company. I was in charge of all its financial aspects, from receiving invoices to preparing salaries and management reports. Each quarter, the interns from a public accounting firm arrived and audited me. Once, an intern said a few sentences that remain etched in my memory: "It's a joke that I'm auditing you. You could teach me! The entire system's upside down. First, I have to do what you're doing. Only then can I audit you."

He was right.

Fifteen years have passed since then, and his words still ring true.

After leaving the firm where I interned, I worked mostly in the field of bookkeeping and private accounting. It's considered dull, and not so glamorous, but, with time, I've discovered that dealing with bookkeeping was precisely what has turned me into a better CPA. Today, I understand accounting processes and can read financial reports much more thoroughly due to my bookkeeping background. I'm certain that such knowledge can prevent quite a few mistakes - and embezzlement.

If you made it so far, dear readers, you're probably asking yourselves why all this is your concern at all. However, this matter concerns almost every person in the world.

Almost every one of us has invested in a public company in some form, whether through our private bank account or through a pension fund. In fact, we're all stockholders; we all need the faithful services of public accountants; and we all want them to know how to perform their work properly.

The sums of money that we set aside are intended to help us when we need them. Our public accountants are our guard dogs, and we want them to know how to guard our money in the best possible manner.

One last little thing:

If you are reading these lines, you have probably finished reading the book and I hope your reading experience was pleasant.

If you enjoyed the read, I would be very grateful if you would take another minute of your time and leave a positive review on the book's Amazon page.

Thank you for reading me
Michal

ABOUT THE AUTHOR

Michal Hartstein was born in 1974 in Israel into a religious family, studied economics and accounting at the University of Tel Aviv and started a career in finance.

In 2006, after becoming a mother, she decided to change direction and began to write. For several years, she has written a popular personal blog, and in 2011 published her first book, *Confession of an Abandoned Wife*. After two years she published her second book, *Hill of Secrets*. In 2014 she participated in the Israeli Nanowrimo contest and wrote *Déjà Vu*. The book was one of the winners and was published in Israel in 2015. Her fourth book, *The Hit*, (the second book in the Hadas Levinger series) was published in 2018.

Ms. Hartstein's books vividly describe the life of the Israeli middle class, focusing on middle class women.